*IN*QUESTOR TALES

Despatches from the High Inquest • Number Five •
June, 2020
Diplodocus Press • Bangkok • Los Angeles

Contents

Message from the High Inquest
In My End is My Beginning

The Homeworld of the Heart - Conclusion
Goddess in the Ruins
by S. P. Somtow

Stillness in Starlight - Part One
The Third Doppling
by S. P. Somtow

Origin Stories
by S.P. Somtow

A Conlang in the Time Before Conlangs
by S.P. Somtow

Lost Tales
Darktouch
by S.P. Somtow

Introduction to *Light on the Sound*
by Darrell Schweitzer

The Inquestor Series
List of Titles

ISBN: 978-1-940999-49-4
Diplodocus Press
Bangkok • Los Angeles
www.diplodocuspress.com

I0620965

Message from the High Inquest

In My End Is My Beginning

Yes, my friends, this issue of *Inquestor Tales* contains the final chunk of *Homeworld of the Heart*. But I'm happy to tell you that it's not *all* it contains.

When I got to the end of the book, I couldn't stop myself. I charged straight ahead and started writing the sixth volume of the "trilogy" — and the first chunk of that is also here.

No, please don't stop.

There are only about 100 people collecting *Inquestor Tales* according to my figures. But those people will end up with all sorts of material that won't be available anywhere else.

For instance, this issue contains the non-canonic original version of the story *Darktouch*, which was subsumed into the novel *The Darkling Wind* with a change of characters and emphasis; this version here was removed from circulation and not reprinted in any anthologies or collections in order not to obscure the Inquestors' official new timeline.

The complete *Homeworld* came out about a month ago. I'm so happy that the handful of readers who have been waiting anxiously for the book seem to be happy.   I will do my best to get the next volume, *Stillness in Starlight*, done in a timely manner as well, but meanwhile you will be getting the serialized early draft in each edition of *Inquestor Tales*.

What is going on?   It took five years to piece together the fifth *Inquestor* novel, but something happened to me, perhaps in part as a result of the Covid-19 crisis ... the weeks of semi-hibernation.

I managed to write the last hundred pages of so of *Homeworld* and my mind ran on and on, so that I also wrote the first fifty pages of the *next* book in the series, and added a pile of index cards to my Inquestor Scrivener folder, figured out more of the language, and wrote more of Sajit's poetry.

— Somtow

CHRONICLES OF THE HIGH INQUEST
Homeworld of the Heart

by S.P. Somtow

Part V
GODDESS IN THE RUINS

Eighteen

The Collecting Field

Where once a crystal needle had threaded the sky, there were now shards, pylons, balconies leaning at impossible angles.

When the flying veranda docked, Sajit's father whispered, "Why did you bring me here? You can only save me, or Tijas."

"No, Starry Highness and Father. I can do both."

Sajit knew that if he could bring himself to the requisite state of mind, there was a way to find Tijas quickly. He would need to enter the space between spaces. Then he could find Tijas immediately — even *before* immediately, because the place he sought was outside spacetime. He knew he could do it. He *had* to do it.

As the veranda slid into place, servocorpses came now, erecting a healing tent around the Princeling.

"Go now," said Orifec weakly, "find your doppling."

Stepped from the balcony into a twisted corridor, and found a displacement plate.   He sat down, emptying his thoughts, crossing his legs and entering *savézhata.*

Tijas! he cried out with his mind.
***

She had not been able to resist coming back. Each day, in the park, there was the same procession. The finding-birds landing and depositing their children, frightened or resigned, excited or placid as servocorpses.

What else did she have to live for? The children of her womb were dead. Her husband was dead. Her planet was dying as it was slowly being ingested by another.

Each day she waited at by the pathway to the quincunx. The crowd thinned each day. They must have found most of the children.   What did not diminish was the pomp, the spectacle, the music pouring out of the sky, the Inquestral anthem shrilling from the heavens.

Above it all, a delphinoid filled half the sky, making the world both day and night at the same time.
***

Cloaked in shadow, another woman came to the

the field.   She had made her way back to the city
easily enough; there were still displacement plates
that worked, here and there, and she knew many
secret subvocalizations that were taught only to the
highest initiates in the temple. She moved among the
throng, pulling as much shadow about her as her
robes could generate, though they had not been
recharged since the temple.

As she was cloaked in shadow, few noticed her,
certainly none of the new denizens of the world that
was no longer Urna.

But the people of Shirenzang could tell when she
approached.   Something fluttering.   Something
shimmering. A tree's shadow, darker than it should
be. Though they saw only shadows, they moved out
of her way. Instinctively, you knows when a god is
present, you know to keep a certain distance. She
would be seen, when she so chose.

And now, she did so choose. There was someone
she needed to speak to.
     ***

Ina desAreon felt only the woman's breath at first;
when she turned there was no one there.

Look harder, said a voice within. *I am near.*

And then another voice — not in her mind. "Ina
desAreon. We have met, in another world."

"You are … the woman cloaked in shadow," Ina said.   "The real mother.   The mother and the goddess."

Ina squinted and could make out very little.   A shimmering, a flutter, a flitting shadow.

"Ina desAreon," came the voice that was right beside her, "our world is fading.   Why have you come here?"

"I want to catch a glimpse of Sajit."

"How do you know he'll come here?"

"The same way you know, goddess."

The music was beginning again.   The crowd leaned forward against the barrier.   Ahead, the five-sided pyramid loomed; they were all in its shadow as Urna's red sun started to set.   The loons were silent.

"It isn't really him, you know," Éluma said.

"Does it matter anymore?" said Ina.   "I know that the doppling kit was activated.   I don't know if I'll see Sajit or —"

"That obscene *thing*," said the goddess.

"And I don't think we'll really be able to tell them apart.   Really.   Goddess — I lost my husband.   I lost my two daughters.   I lost the world I lived in.   A shadow of my Sajit would be better than nothing."

"It's not what we believe in."

"I don't think anyone cares what we believe in, anymore," Ina said.   "I don't think anyone cares if we even exist."

"But what if *everyone* made copies of the people they loved?   Wouldn't life have no more meaning? Wouldn't you just be able to replace one child with another that was exactly the same?   Would you shed tears if he died?   If you could just open a box and bring put another one out? What about the sanctity of life?"

"Everyone *hasn't* made copies of everybody else," said Ina.   "We are just talking about one person. And it's a person we both love."

"But *a* person Not two."

"Goddess, I know that if I see my boy again, I won't care if he's only a shadow's shadow of my son."

Now the crowd surged.   Ina found herself pushed against the barrier.   For a moment she thought she could see the woman's face.

But the goddess folded herself back in shadow.
***

The spectacle was beginning.   A squadron of childsoldiers led the way, beating back the throng. On a hoverfloat came drummers, pounding on man-tall drums covered in human skin, their flayed faces flopping down their edges.

Breaching the clouds, a flock of finding-birds swooped down, each deposit a child in the middle of the walkway.   The children stumbled forward, urged on by childsoldiers.

Mikkálu was there too. But he had not expected to see Éluma in the crowd. He tried not to see her, but, pushing against the barrier, her face emerged out of the darkweave that she wore.

"I said goodbye already," Mikkálu said. "I said I'd come for you one day."   Why couldn't this have ended cleanly, like a servocorpse drama, in neat little segments?

The woman who was standing next to Éluma said, "Who is this boy? Do you know him? How do you know a childsoldier?"

Mikkálu could see that there were stories within stories here — doorways that should not be opened. He needed to slam them shut. The Child Collector would be waiting for his equerry.

The woman reached through the barricade, gripped Mikkálu's arm. "You know the woman cloaked in shadow," she whispered. "You know *something*. Do you know my son? Do you know Sajit?"

"Your *son?*" But before Mikkálu had time to react, another finding-bird plummeted down and disgorged Tijas. Bewildered, unkempt, his clingfire ripped, the boy had landed right in the middle of the procession.

He held aloft a ring with an intagliate pattern of serpents and he shouted "It's me, it's me, I'm the real one, take *me!*"

The strange woman beat at the barricade with her fists. "Sajit, Sajit," she screamed, "let me through to him!"

Mikkálu grasped Tijas's arm. His fist was a boy's but his training was a soldier's.

"You killed my father," Tijas shrieked, "let go!"

"Your father —" said the woman Mikkálu did not know, "Your father was crushed to death when the people bins fell from the sky!"

"Ina, I'm not your son, I am Tijas."

"I don't care who you are! You belong with me!"

And then Sajit was there too, materializing out of nowhere, falling out of nothing into Tijas's arms.

The sight of twins — abomination, in broad daylight, was a shock. People around them were making signs of aversion or reciting mantras. A man bent down to find a rock to hurl. Another was already throwing a stone but in an instant Mikkálu looked up and pulverised it with a laser glance. The crowd was screaming, back away.

"No stone throwing!" Childsoldiers were in crowd control mode, barking at the the crowd and quirting them.

   ***

"I knew that I could save you," Sajit said. "I knew I could leap through the space between spaces and find you."

Ina said, "You've come back to me."

"No, mother. I've come to take my doppling's place. Take him. Love him. You never really loved me anyway — I wasn't really yours. But you can atone for that. You can love Tijas."

"I think I can," Ina said.

And once more Éluma was shrieking — *"Abomination! Abomination!"* ripping the darkweave that girded her, baring the bosom of the goddess to the crowd. She was flinging herself against the barrier. Ina was trying to hold her back —

"How could you reject him?" Ina screamed. "From a womb or from a box, *your* DNA!"

Éluma rent the darkweave. Her breasts emerged from the fabric of darkness. As she raved, darkness billowed about her, showing that which humans may not see, except when celebrating the most sacred of all mysteries.

"Aërat!" Some crowd members were crying out, some falling to their knees, some shielding the eyes of their children.

"I have birthed a living twin!" Éluma cried. "I'm forever defiled, no goddess — I'm a whore!"

Wailing, shrieking, she flung herself against the barrier. Ina caught her, took her in her arms. "You'll always be the goddess," she said.

***

Consternation was spreading. Sajit could see that he and Tijas were being pointed at, laughed at, reviled. He could see the two mothers, one raving, the other trying to comfort.

"One of us has to die," he said.

He turned away from his mothers.

"And it's going to be me," Tijas said.

The path to the quincunx, perhaps a half klomet, was lined with citizens of Urna and curiosity-seekers from Alykh. But those nearby, just across the barrier ,were already recoiling.

He remembered, from his childhood, the nightmare —

The ritual stoning of the twin —

Sajit ran.

But Tijas ran too.

Neck and neck, feeling each other's footfall, in perfect synchronicity, the ran. Past gaping children, chiding old women, stern childsoldiers.

Stoning the twin —

The memory came. Each time his feet pounded the paving, he saw a stone whistling and the crowd roaring out its deep, hungry mantra —

Life is sacred.

Life is one.

Life is not two.

Two is abomination.

Above them, Mikkálu wheeled on his hoverdisk. He somersaulted. He shrieked out the childsoldier's warcry, egging them on. They ran, their thoughts bouncing back and forth.

Sajit remembering —

Tijas whispering in his mind: *That is not my nightmare. That is* yours, *Sajit.*

Then I must remember for both of us, Sajit thought.

The rock smashing the baby's skull...

They ran.

At the foot of the escalator childsoldiers stepped out to block their path. "One at a time."

Sajit pushed his brother, tried to knee him off the upper step — the childsoldiers tried to separate them until Mikkálu spoke to them. The escalator moved up, slowly. The dopplings didn't speak. Each was trying to shove the other off the escalator. There was no railing and the the drop would be steep. As the escalator moved higher, they became more careful with each other.

Sajit did not want to kill his brother. But he had to get ahead.

They gripped each other tight. They were sweating, slippery, and the moving escalator precarious. They embraced in violence and love. They were deadlocked. They ascended. The plateau-like parapet hove into view, and at its top, the Child Collector waited, maniples of childsoldiers perched on their whirling hoverdisks, while above them, like the snakes that symbolized the royal house of Urna, twisting, writhing tubes that were sucking up children into the sky.

Mikkálu ran ahead, all the way to Gharém, who stood, impassive. Mikkálu did not know what to say, how to get out of the situation.

"My Lord!" Mikkálu cried out. "I'm sorry it took so long — but I've come back with your prize — twofold."

***

Kyar Gharém was not fond of surprises. The Collection was supposed not supposed to have hitches. Seeing the equerry disheveled and out of breath, he reacted by slapping him sharply.

"My Lord!" Mikkálu gasped. "Did you really need to do that? I'm not one of your servocorpse lovers."

Gharém resisted the impulse to strike him again. "I give you a *lot* of leeway," he said, "because your impertinence amuses me. But know your place."

"Kyar Gharém, I've brought you your prize trophy. But as you can see, he's been doppled."

"Well, what is that to me? Dispose of one. The count must be correct."

"You want me to randomly kill one?" Mikkálu said. Gharém, in this kind of mood, always felt a bit contrary.   Perhaps, he thought, the equerry was playing him.

"No, of course not," Gharém said, "the Inquest is compassionate. Send one back."

"My brother will go back," the twins both said.

"Dopplings," Gharém said.   "According to this world's traditions, one twin is always slain at birth. Only their royal family is allowed the privilege of doppling and therefore the twins would not be identical, but disparate in age. We have, it seems, an anomaly."

"Lord Gharém, they *are* of the royal family," Mikkalu said.

"Then let them show their humanity."

Gharém clapped his hands and space was cleared. The childiers formed a five-sided space. Above them, the suction tubes hovered, hissing as they twisted, the necks of a monstrous hydra.

"We'll have a little contest. Which of you loves the other more? Who will sacrifice himself? You shall fight — and the one who remains conscious — *he* will be adjudged the better childsoldier. The other will be thrown back to earth — a Princeling without a country — as worthless as dust."

***

Tijas whispered, "Go limp when I hit you. Then I'll run up to the tubes —"

He didn't finish his sentence. Sajit had already punched him. Tijas reeled, thinking, *How did you hide your intentions from me?* — and Sajit was running toward the center of the pentagon.

Childsoldiers began a rhythmic chanting —

shashashasha há há! shashashasha há há!

shrill, elemental, terrifying. They rattled their hoverdisks against their sides, the slap of metal on hard young flesh sounding *chaka chaka chaka* against the keening of their warcry.

No! Tijas leaped, tackled his twin — Sajit's forehead thudded on the flagstones and Tijas tasted blood, he knew he was feeling what his brother felt, the pain radiating our from above his eyes —

Tijas ran toward the center of the parapet, where the quincuncial archway waited.

The childsoldiers moved in formation, metal boots clanging against the stones. Narrowing the area, step by step, they chanted —

shashash sha há há! shashashasha há há!
shashash sha há há! shashashasha há há!

Tijas cried out into Sajit's mind: *I'm stronger than you because this is my* meúr. *You can't stop me. I was made to take your place.*

Sajit pulled himself together. He sprang, tripped his twin; they both fell, feeling each other's pain as they grazed the pavement, feeling the feedback loop of the pain as it echoed back and forth — pain in waves, bounding and rebounding.   Sajit pushed himself up.   Tijas was nearing the center of the quincunx, and the tubes from the sky were coming together, ready to draw their prey into the sky.

Sajit leaped.   He tripped Tijas and sent him sprawling. "Powers of powers, Sajitteh! Just let me do what I'm here to do!" But now Sajit had Tijas in a wrestling hold. The pain they felt, each other's pain, tinged with love and heartbreak — it was unbearable. They were both weeping. And the childsoldiers were moving in, chanting and banging their hoverdisks. The suction tube was closing in. He could feel the air emptying around him. For a moment he wavered —

And suddenly it was Tijas who had him pinned down.

And the childsoldiers were laughing.   Tijas saw mockery. He saw the Child Collector, self-satisfied, whisper in Mikkálu's ear.

He felt his brother's pain — his regret — and the terrible love his brother felt which amplified itself over and over as it bounced back and forth through their echo chamber minds —

One of us has to let go, he said in his mind. *Or the pain will kill us both.*

At that moment, the childsoldier barrier split open. Two women pushed their way through, and the childsoldiers did not stop them.

One was Ina, the not-mother who had not even known of Tijas's existence before today.

The other, with only a few strips of shadow clinging to her perfect divine body, was the goddess — the mother who could not accept him.

They were weeping. They had fought. Somehow, they had achieved a kind of concord. "Come home, Sajit," said Ina. "Come home, Sajit," said the goddess of love.

But they're not saying my *name*, Tijas thought.

A wave of desolation, of aloneness, overwhelmed and his grip slipped.

I am a monster, Tijas thought.

"No!" Sajit cried aloud. "You're not a monster, you'll never be a monster — how could you be, when I'm willing to die for you?"

And Sajit stretched his head toward the sky and the writhing tubes caught him, and tendriled around him, and held him fast, jerking him up into the air and into the maw of the sucking tunnel that stretched all the way to the delphinoid in the sky —

In Tijas's mind — silence.

The connection was broken.

Tijas could not feel his doppling anymore.

The pain was ebbing, replaced by an still more terrible numbness.

***

There were no downward escalators from the Quincunx of Collection. It was designed as a one-way journey. Thus it was that while the childsoldiers and the Child Collector immediately turned their attention toward the new line of recruits advancing up the escalator — a line that was beginning to stabilize now that the scuffle was over — Tijas found himself face to face with the two women — not knowing whether he should embrace them or fear them.

"You say you love me," he said. "But neither of you would say my name."

Ina tried to reach out. But Éluma turned her back … in a way that Tijas had seen before.…

In Sajit's nightmare. The stoning, and the Woman Cloaked in Shadow turning her back.…

Tijas looked away from the two women.

Only Mikkálu paid heed to them, and he did so with one eye on his master, who might summon him to his side at any moment.

How could he look at Éluma, when he'd killed the father of her child … while trying to kill her child? … Nothing could ever be the same again.

And Ina … what was she to the child he almost killed?

A childsoldier is pitiless.

Tijas tried to reach out to Sajit but it was if a wall had sprung up between their minds. Something inside the tubes … or perhaps some force radiating from the delphinoid shipmind that hung overhead.

Never, since he first came out of the box, had Tijas felt so desolate. Behind him, children moved in five sets of single file towards the center, and one by one they were being sucked into the star whale's belly.

The Child Collector motioned Mikkálu over and said, "Send them away. They're a blot on the beauty of this ritual."

Mikkálu subvoked a quick command and a mobile displacement plate pushed its way up through the floor of the pentagon. A floater materialized in the space … a maniple-sized floater, military issue, used in the ambushing of cities.

"Go where you want to go," he said. "The High Inquest doesn't need you anymore."

And they went.

***

Mikkálu watched the goddess stumble toward the displacement plate, helped by the village woman who had raised her child. The displacement plate vanished in a halo of blue light.

Mikkálu did not want to weep again; excessive tears could misalign the laser-irises in his eyes. The railing of the palace parapet was peppered with holes from his tears. He could not have his eyes go out of alignment. Better to pluck them out. Childsoldiers do not make such errors.

He had already misfired once. There could never be another.

He was glad Kyar Gharém did not yet know....

"As for you, my impertinent little equerry," Gharém said, "I seem to have cut you a lot of slack. You have been my favorite equerry, precisely because you are hard to cow, you're unorthodox. But this time you've gone too far."

"I'm sorry, my Lord."

"Get out of my sight," said the Child Collector. "I'll chastise you in my own good time."

Mikkálu clenched back a terrible anger.

Nineteen

Princelings and Goddesses

The floater had brought them to the lowest level of Nevéqilas. They had not said a word to one another. When the reached the base of the crystal flower, the boy who so resembled Sajit strode purposefully away, and Ina did not know where he was going.

The floater left them, standing amid the rubble and the shattered crystal that had been their world.

Urna's star hung dim behind violent-fringed clouds. There were two pale moons.

"He's going to his father," said Éluma.

"His father is dead," said Ina desAreon. But it rang false; she knew her son and his doppling had had another life as well, other parents.

"I mean the Princeling," said Éluma.

"Should I follow?" Ina said.

"How could you?" said the goddess. "You are just some villager. And his father is a Starry Highness."

"But you do not follow? His father may be a princeling, but you are a goddess."

"Not any more."

Ina said, "There are so few of us left. Surely we've got to find a way to … find some kind of peace."

"Peace?" Éluma cried. "I caused Orifec's death! I turned my back on my child!"

"But there was abomination. You had no choice."

"Oh, I was blind," Éluma said, and she wept bitterly.

***

When Tijas reached the palace, a speaking boy-corpse had been waiting; he was led to a room that could be reached only through displacement … a garden of glass, a field of clear crystal pebbles. He found the Princeling surrounded by servocorpses — functioning as medics, orderlies, and courtiers.

Orifec lay under a canopy of a a glass tree that grew in the center of the chamber — a chamber that seemed infinite because its walls reflected each other infinitely.

"Where am I?" he asked the corpse.

"This is called Véravur," the corpse said. "It's the Princeling's chamber of dying and remembrance." The boy said, "Let the Rememberers enter now."

Tijas went to Orifec's bedside. Half his body was submerged in an amniosis balm, but his head and part of his torso could be seen. The iatromaton mad cooing sounds as its tentacles touched the Princeling and read vital signs. He had been shaved.

"Ah, Tijas," Orifec said.

"How can you tell us apart?" Tijas said.

Orifex said, "Perhaps a lucky guess. Or perhaps, as possessor of half your DNA, I'm just better at guessing than other people." A frown, briefly. "Tijas, you must not be afraid I am in pain. I know you're thinking that. In fact I am buoyed up by so many opiates that though I'm severed in two, and my functions are all grinding to a halt, I … still speak, cogently, even volubly."

Tijas smiled. "The goddess, my real mother, has gone mad because of me. And as for my foster-mother — I don't know what she thinks."

"She'll come round." Orifec said. "They both will. Our ancient civilization is no more — there's no need to cling to superstitions."

"Honestly, Starry Highness — did you *really* know it was me?"

"I guess," said Orifec. "But I guessed with good logic."

"Why?"

The glass fronds tinkled. A soft breeze came; servocorpses were fanning them with the feathers of firephoenixes. Above, the moons danced. Holosculpts-views to be sure. The room was a womb.

"I know you would both to anything to save the other. But Sajit is the elder. I know that the elder will always sacrifice to preserve the younger — I know this because I am myself a doppling, and I have the memories of generations of dopplings."

"I understand, father." He did not really understand how any emotion of Sajit's could be more powerful than his own. But he tried to listen to every world Orifec said. He knew already that this would be their last time together. He sat down on the soft meniscus of the amniofluid.

"I would have welcomed either of you," Orifec said. "But one of you *had* to come. I could not wait for ever. I'm barely holding on — you cannot tell, because I am in no pain. But I must anoint the next Princeling. And I must give you all my — *our* memories."

Rememberers were materializing around them, all in the white robes that signified their calling. They were all ancient, wizened men and women, their brains stuffed, no doubt, with generational histories.

"Do I have to listen to them *all?*" Tijas said, bewildered.

Orifec managed a wry smile. "That would take lifetimes," he said softly. "They are just here as part of the ritual. Do you know why you have to be here, Tijas?"

"I think so," Tijas said, but he didn't like the answer.

Orifec wants me to succeed him.

"I'm not your doppling," Tijas said, "and I don't have a planet to rule over."

"That is true," Orifec said, "but I can't die until I pass on all these remembrances. Or they, too, will die."

The chief Rememberer held a glass dish in his hands, on which there writhed a little green worm ...

"Tash Tonadár," Orifec whispered. The Rememberer's name and clan-name.

And Tijas knew that the worm would be the conduit, boring into Orifec's skull to extract his memories ... and to transfer them to his own....

The Rememberer picked the work from the dish and it started to lengthen, its segments multiplying until it coiled again and again around the Rememberer's wrist....

Tijas cried out, "I don't want memories ... I want to *forget!*"

"I know you do," said the Rememberer whom Orifec had called Tonadár.   "And yet ... you are empty now. And your mind needs filling."

Tijas said, "How can I explain this emptiness? Sajit was with me every second of my life. We *were* each other."

Tonadár said, "Those delphinoid shipminds ... they cast a psychic interference field that blocks a lot what goes on in a human mind. It was not aimed at you specifically. It is because when humans travel in the light-mad overcosm, they can be driven insane unless their thoughts are a little dulled."

"Will I sense him again, then?"

"That I don't know.   The connection between dopplings is not well understood."

But we reached out to each other even in the space between spaces! Tijas thought.

"Perhaps, when the shipmind has reached its destination, you will feel him again."

"I'll have to hope," Tijas said.

Thus it was that he did not resist when the servocorpses started to shave his head and when the worm of remembrance was placed on his scalp and began to burrow....

***

And Ina made her way back to the ruins of her home. Now there was truly nothing to live for. She sat in a corner for a day, perhaps many days, not eating … around her, the holosculpt projector played landscapes on shuffle, switching from cityscapes to ice deserts to spiralling mountains and scarlet snows, the views fading from one to another. At length, their repertoire played out, the walls blanked; still she sat.

She did not remember eating, though she must have. She only sat, remembering moments from before

After a measureless time, a young dead page displaced into the room. He wore a tunic of shimmerfur, knotted with a belt of mating serpents; she knew that he came from the palace.

He handed her a message disk, which said to her, in a soft, childlike voice, *The Starry Highness requests the presence of Ina desAreon.*

Confused, numb, she followed him.

***

She was a shell. Weeping had drained her of all feeling.

She did not know how long she walked, how many times she crossed the same street to find it different every time. Her feet had lost their covering and only pieces of the darkness that cloaked her remained.

But in the end, she found herself at the entrance to the Temple of Aërat. And the corpses who guarded the gate still knew her, though she was naked, filthy, even bloodstained.

And they called her "Goddess."

They took her to her quarters, cleansed her, perfumed her, and gave her a new cloak of shadow. They painted her face and lined her eyes, and reddened her lips and rouged her nipples.

The temple was full of tourists; there were few real worshippers now. When she left her dressing chamber, some tourists recognized her from the holosculpt images that were everywhere. Some did a mocking obeisance — oh, they did not know they mocked, but thought they were participating in some quaint, picturesque ritual.

In a courtyard, goddesses in training danced to the twang of an untuned kítharon. Their finger-cymbals clicked in time to the batting of eyelashes, and they pointed their feet daintily.

An acolyte held up a reflector and she saw herself and she thought … *I look almost like myself.*

A dead page met her in one of the gardens and told her that the Starry Highness was asking for her presence.

"But isn't he —"

"You'll see, Goddess."

***

There was a garden all of glass, a garden without doors, accessible only by displacement.

One by one, important guests were materializing on the plates the rimmed the chamber. Éluma had never heard of this room, did not even know where it was; at its center there was a tree, all glass, with tinkling leaves, branching all the way to infinity, though she did not know if the reflective crystal of the ceiling was a holosculpt.

The people in the room were dressed in their palatial best — incongruously perhaps, since they were the elite of a civilization that was barely clinging to existence. Éluma saw a few other divinities — though Love was the most venerated on Urna, there were lesser deities, all represented in the world by their human embodiments. The Death God was there, his hair aflame and his nude body painted completely white, his four arms undulating, with a servocorpse on a leash. The God of War was present too, a mechanical in the shape of a childsoldier, whose joints clanked, metal on metal.

Then there were nobles … Éluma recognized them from their visits to the temple … she knew some of them quite intimately, knew their arcane requirements when celebrating the rituals of love.

Beneath the glassy canopy, on a crystal throne, sat … the abomination that was like her son.

In front of him, in a crystal sarcophagus, afloat in an opiate bath, was the torso of the Princeling who had once been her lover. The two were connected, shaved head to shaved head, by a tendriling, twisting annelid that had burrowed into both their skulls. The worm quivered and undulated.

Behind them stood a row of Rememberers, in the white robes of the Clan of Ton.

A few servocorpses moved about the chamber, trayfloats at their fingertips, serving chasers of concentrated *zul* and canapés made from chocolate and flowers. But no one was eating or drinking.

Éluma knew the ceremony ... knew it from the tellers of history, for she could not have been present at the last one. It was an accession ceremony. And *Tijas*, the Abomination, was going to be Princeling.

The woman Ina desAreon was beside her suddenly. Éluma had not noticed her before. The woman was not dressed for the occasion but wore a shapeless stola fastened with crystal brooch. She seemed to have come straight from the invitation without having stopped to make herself look presentable; either she did not know the protocol for a princeling's invitation, or she had nothing to wear.

Éluma did not wish to speak to her, even to acknowledge her. The emotions that had passed between them in the Collecting Quincunx were too painful to relive. But Ina came closer, refusing to melt into the crowd.

"Please," she said. "I don't know anyone here. Please … goddess."

"Not any more," Éluma said bitterly. "You've seen what I am."

Ina reached out to her. She found herself clasping Ina's hand. With a strange desperation. And then the voice came.

It was the voice of Orifec, yet not his voice. *I am the Son of the Starlight, the High Princeling Orifec z'Urnasi Tath, hereditary Lord of Nevéqilas, Commander of the World Entire, He Who Answers Only to the High Inquest.*

The voice did not come from where Orifec lay, but was broadcasting from the walls, the floor, the ceiling itself, a sound both human and brittle, like glass itself.

To me alone is vouchsafed the forbidden. I have died and returned many times over. In me is the wisdom of my previous selves. It is our tradition.

But our world is ending, and our civilization must evolve now. Urna is falling beyond. *And thus it is that we shall break tradition. My memories will not go to a doppling but to a changeling.*

He is young, but inside him will be the voices of Starry Highnesses going all the way back to the first. Obey him as you would me; for I live again in him.

Now you will witness this child, born from the union of Goddess and Princeling, as he slays his father and becomes the new Son of the Starlight, the High Princeling Tijassah darOrifec z'Urnasi Tath, Who Answers Only to the High Inquest.

A gasp. This was inconceivable.

But in a moment, Tijas had yanked the worm from Orifec's forehead. A strangled cry escaped the princeling's throat … and then a death-rattle … amplified by the crystals of the chamber, so that the branches shook and the crystals tinkled and the whole chamber seemed to howl.

The crystal coffin containing the dead princeling wavered a little, blinking in and out of existence. Then it vanished, displacing to the secret, orbiting mnemothanasion that was the burial place of all Starry Highnesses.

A chill came over the chamber. The Rememberers, the guests, even the servocorpses fell to the ground in prostration. Even the gods inclined their heads.

And so it was that Éluma found herself still standing amid a sea of backs.

And it seemed that the only other person standing was Ina desAreon.

Tijas said, "Mothers, come to me."

Éluma threaded her way through the still-prostrate throng. The suppliants shifted, parted, making a pathway. A few steps behind, Ina too was approaching.

Tijas came down from the glazen throne. The two women stood in front of him. He said, "I didn't choose this. It should have been Sajit."

Ina said, "I know, Starry Highness. This is why the doppling kit was brought to our home. We always knew that there would be a culling of childsoldiers. We didn't dream there would be a *falling beyond.*"

Éluma said, "But I didn't know. Nobody warned me. Nobody prepared me."

"And how could they have, mother," said Tijas, "knowing that you are the living goddess, the emblem of all that this world stands for, the guardian of all its traditions?"

"We made Sajit out of our love," Éluma said. "I had no rôle in making you at all. Orifec planned to defy tradition. I never really understood."

Tijas said, "But now, only one of you can be my mother. And I can't be the one to choose."

Twenty

The Goddess in the Ruins

Tijas dimissed the throng. One by one they filed to displacement plates and blinked out. Now only the three remained. Tijas returned to the throne and sat down again. He deopaqued the walls and ceiling and now it seemed as though the were on a sea of glass, beneath the clear night sky of Urna, under the singing moons. Only the crystal tree and throne remained from the garden of glass.

Tijas was alone with the two women who were not his mother.

Two women who could never understand his bereavement, his emptiness.

He sat, the worm wound round his shaved head. It was shrinking now, and soon it would be completely absorbed into his brain.

Already there were alien memories and thoughts — whispers, contradictions. He was beginning to know the weight that rested on Orifec's mind all the time. Memories of murders and lovers and disappointments ... memories of being both the traitor and the betrayed.

He was his father, holding the child Sajit, feeling his father's dream of breaking away from the past.

He was Orifec in the forest, hearing Sajit's voice for the first time, swelling with pride and sadness ... already foreseeing the coming of the Child Collector. ...

He was Orifec again in the Room of the Clouds and Rain ... making love to the Goddess ... he was the pinprick consciousness of a single sperm cell swimming upstream ... the moment of Sajit's conception — he was there, he was inside his own mother....

I'll go mad! he was thinking.

He pulled at the worm with his hand, staying its progress. The voices grew quieter.

He looked at the Goddess and felt what Orifec felt when he first saw her. He could see her conflicted feelings — her love for Sajit, her gut loathing of Abomination — and most of all her guilt. He saw the Goddess in a thousand ways, for behind this goddess there were other goddesses seen by other Orifecs as well, all the way to the beginning.

He looked at Ina, who had lost everything. Her face was weathered and aged not by time but by suffering. But in her eyes, he saw, there was the dawning of a kind of love.

Again he tugged at the worm. Its loose end writhed and spiralled against his skin. A greenish rheum dripped from the tail end which had been plugged into his father's skull.

"Oh, mothers who are not my mothers," he said. "What future is there for us?"

***

"I killed him," Éluma said. "I killed the Starry Highness." Once again, as she before in the quincunx, she was weeping uncontrollably, lashing out with her arms. Ina tried to hold her still.

"But you were trying to kill *me*," Tijas said.

"And I broke Mikkálu's heart."

"Yes, you did. You gave him an impossible choice." Tijas was implacable.

"I killed Sajit, too. I killed my child."

"You don't know that."

"Yes I do. There's an emptiness. You know it. You feel it."

"You don't know it, Éluma. He may survive being a childsoldier. You know the ancient ditty."

"Yes. *A million young boys dreamed of the stars ... one hundred thousand became childsoldiers ... ninety-nine thousand died ... one became an Inquestor.*"

... a song that children sing when passing the time on long journeys.

"I'm all you have left. Yet you rejected me. But then again, we never had a connection. Do you know how many times I joined the family for breakfast — and Sajit was watching from concealment, laughing? You never knew, never guessed. There was nothing to reject." She felt his sadness, far more hurtful than anger would have been.

Éluma said, "I can't solve this. I'm broken, and nothing can put me together again."

"Then go where you wish. It was my thought to reestablish the long-forgotten position of Valydé, the Princeling's Mother, but I see you will not accepted it."

Tijas summoned a servocorpse with a wave of his hand. He told it to lead the Goddess wherever she wished to go.

***

Ina was the only guest left in the room, save for servocorpses.

"I'll be your mother, Tijas," she said at last.

"I know," Tijas said.

"How?"

"I know everything Orifec knew. I know why this family was chosen, this village. And you knew about the doppling kit all along, and you didn't … abhor it."

"I can tell you things about yourself … your other self … that even you don't know," Ina said. "Come down from that throne."

"I've got a worm trying to burrow itself into me."

"Hold on to it … pull at it, slow it down. Once it's in there, you really will be the Starry Highness. You will be my Lord. And you will be every Princeling of Urna before you. But for now … you're still … the shadow of my son."

"Tell me one of these things I don't know," Tijas said.

The boy was no Princeling, not yet. Ina saw a frail, frightened child. She thought of Sajit, in the hold of the delphinoid shipmind, perhaps in stasis, about to travel for who knows how long.   But she could still see her son in Tijas's eyes.

"He used to wake up from a nightmare," she said. "I used to think it was fantasy, but now I know it was premonition ... foreshadowing."

This is the story she told Tijas....
***

He would come to me in the night, in a cold sweat, and he would say ... they're stoning me.   And I would say Who? Who?

And he said, Everyone we know. They're in a circle. They're throwing stones.   Smashing my face, my skull, oh, mother, it hurts, hurts. *And I said it's just a dream.   But I knew better.*

When Sajit was a toddler there was a doppling-stoning in the village.   And he witnessed it....

I should have let him sleep.   I didn't know.   I took him from his bed and held him in my arms at first but he was getting heavy now.   I let him walk.   He let go my hand.   He toddled ahead.

These ceremonies have long been outlawed. Devivement is supposed to be painless.   But this child's family was religious.   They needed to see the death for themselves, to make sure the abomination was truly rooted out.

He saw me cast the stone. He picked one up himself and thrust it at the child, though it fell short. They stamped their feet and chanted age-old curses.

When he threw the rock I threw my arms around him and took him back inside.

From time to time, he would dream of it … but I told him it was only a nightmare.

He was four years old.

***

Tijas said, "He never showed me this."

He started to cry. Ina took him in her arms. "It will be all right," she told him. "Whatever you do, I'll stand with you."

"I know," said Tijas.

"Will you renounce the kingdom?"

"Kingdom? It's only a memory of a kingdom … yet I'm told we still have the rights to some tiny patches of this planet."

He let go of the memory worm. It slithered inside him. More memories came, crowding, all demanding his attention. But they would never be his own memories. He would never really be Orifec. That was the gift his father had given his kingdom, though the gift had come too late, only in the kingdom's last days: he had moved it from stifling repetition into a time of change. After all these centuries, Urna would be ruled by *someone else* — someone who yet held the memories of the past but could use a new viewpoint to discover fresh truths, fresh paths to travel.

"No, I won't," said Tijas, "not just yet."

***

Éluma reentered the temple, and she summoned all those beneath her: all the gods and goddesses in training, all the stewards, all the pages, even such servocorpses as had been endowed with the capacity for thought and speech.

"I've been here all my life," she said, "and yet I've never seen this temple for what it is."

And she commanded her minions to deopaque all the walls, to shut of the holosculpt generators, to silence the music that had never been silenced. And all of them stood there, gaping at the reality of Aërat's domain.

There were broken columns. Flagstones veined with ancient weeds. A chipped planter with a wilted rosella-tree. There were walls with patches of bright murals — scenes of lovemaking — images so ancient that they did not even move.

"Our world is being subsumed into Alykh," Éluma said. "On Urna what we do is sacred. In Aírang, which they call the City of Love, we are whores. Let us embrace this."

She watched the faces of her acolytes — those that had faces, for the dead only have the simulacrum of a face, without true feeling, and many of the humans had already abandoned the temple. Dead or alive, they wore little expression. She understood — their lives had been divested of all meaning without warning, without reason.

"I want to tell you that I am the last incarnation of the goddess. The goddess is no more. Look around you. It is illusion. It's *always* been illusion."

"But even if it's illusion," said one the stewards, "should we not at least cling to it?"

"Worlds die," Éluma said. "Civilizations collapse. Even the High Inquest itself may fall one day."

That caused a gasp.

"All my life I've known as a fact that the sanctity of the human soul means that we are unique — that to be double is abomination. When … *twins* … occur in our lives, we know what must we done. We do it, the act itself is abhorrent, but we *have* to do it. Just like we have to have children, to die, to make love. Only the Princeling may reproduce by doppling — because state of Princehood is itself unique. Then I learned that my own child was a doppling."

More gasps. The steward said, "I heard a rumor, goddess — some kind of scandal at the Collecting Field."

"No rumor. *Nothing* we knew as fact is true now. Urna is ended."

Éluma had never spoken so many words at one time. Her very godhead depended on mystery. Her sexual power was so refined she could control the very pheromones she exuded. She did not need to speak except in riddles. Her addressing the acolytes, like the proprietress of a bakery or a corpse factory regaling her staff, was a novel thing to do and yet she found herself, in a strange way, enjoying it. They were listening to her, and not because she was repeating a millennia mantra ... because she was struggling to find a pathway that they all must follow.

"This is another world and we must adapt," she said. "We were adapting a little bit, allowing them to enter out sacred halls and gawk at our quaint rituals. But we have to go further."

"How, goddess?" said the steward, pursing her lips.

"These people are merchants. And we have skills they can't even dream of. How many of them can name number the erogenous punctilia of a man's penis? Even a seven-year-old among you acolytes knows how to prolong the suppliant's sweet anguish beyond the point of explosion, to a transcendental union with infinity. Can they do that? Will they not pay for it? We too have something we can sell. After the people bins came, a man named Lang viHurek came here and offered us a contract ... an, to his mind, an entertainment deal. I slapped his face."

The temple, decaying; the walls half crumbled, the holosculpts fragmented and pixellated ... on the unmoving murals, the ancient technology, remained fresh. Thousand-year-old young lovers, in contorted positions, frozen ecstasy ... speaking from the past.

"Follow me," said the goddess. "We are going to find viHurek and make that deal."

The gates of the temple were not gates at all. They had always been an illusion. The temple's roof had caved in since the coming of the people bins.

Éluma stepped through the gates that were not gates.

A pathway led towards what had once been the city center. Beyond it, the new city, Aírang, was still expanding visibly; its skyscrapers were still inching toward the sky, its spider-architects still frantically piling more units on top of units.

"Follow me to the city of pleasure," Éluma said. "In our new existence, we are not deities. We are whores. Embrace that. We have skills that will blindside their imaginations. We'll dazzle their *dorezdas*. We'll remake their world. They call themselves a city of pleasure! We'll show them pleasure! We'll become the thing they are most know for!"

She laughed — a laughter in which each silvery peal was modulated to arouse.

As she said this she began to tear great strips of shadow from her body. Such was her art that the more she revealed, the more she seemed to conceal. The acolytes followed suit, flinging their vestments into the street. Threads of darkness crisscrossed, twirled.

I've lost everything, she thought, *so I might as well be free of everything.*

She began to sing. So this motley parade of naked beauty made its chaotic way down the street, with the corpses hardly less lively than the living, for they were well programmed, to catch exactly the mood of those they were with.

***

Meanwhile, in what had once been the private throneroom of the Princeling of Urna, or more properly the High Princeling Tijassah darOrifec z'Urnasi Tath held court, such as it was.

The governance of Urna had not changed since even before the world had become absorbed into the Dispersal of Man. It had always been a sparsely populated world with but a single land mass, a single major city, and a network of villages. The court of Urna had been mostly ceremonial for generations. Yes, the Princeling wielded absolute power; but custom decreed that the real power was held by deputies and, ultimately, by thinkhives.

The Starry Highness held authority in the name of the High Compassion of the Inquest.

The throneroom was not as it was when Sajit and Tijas had spied on it ... which had not been that long ago. Holosculpt generators were out of sync. But the twined serpent columns were still there — they were real, just giving the illusion of marmáreon.

The court comprised only a few people: a Rememberer whose white robe seemed soiled, as though he had dressed in haste to come to this assembly; the Princely Vizier, a barechested old man in a pointed hat and curly-tipped slippers — someone Tijas had not even known existed; and the usual corpses and scribes.

On his right hand they had set up a seat for Ina, who by default had assumed the millennially obsolete title of Valvdé, the mother of the ruler.

Tijas knew what to do, from the memories he had absorbed. But what he had to do seemed so irrelevant.

The Vizier had begun his daily recitation of the kingdom's assets. "Of land, there remains for your use ... one square klomet."

"That's my whole kingdom?"

"By rules of Inquestral *makrúgh*, when a planet *falls beyond* one square klomet may remain as a living mnemothanasion, Starry Highness. The world Alykh has encroached on everything else ... in law if not in fact ... and within your reserved territory, often in fact though not in law."

"And you don't care, that our whole civilization has been reduced to one square klomet?"

"Should I, Starry Highness? Truth to tell, I've never left the palace. I was born and raised in your service."

"My service?"

"There is but one Starry Highness, ever and always."

"I don't have a world to rule," Tijas said, wondering why he had allowed the worm of memory to slither into his brain at all. He rubbed the pinhole where it had gone in. "What *do* I have? Wealth? Assets?"

"You have immediate liquidity of seven trillion iridas, and some investments off-world. Personal funds, Starry Highness."

"So ... I could, for example, take passage on a delphinoid. I could go off-world, anywhere."

"Indeed."

"And the thinkhives can rule in my name and no one would be the wiser."

"It has generally been so, Starry Highness."

Tijas said, "Then ... soon ... I should go."

Ina said, "Where, my son?"

"I don't know," he said.

Sajit! Still unreachable. Cut off. The aloneness could not be described, not even in music.

Then he started thinking of Daro. And the Professor with the rainbow eyelids. And the tales they told of the lives of wandering actors, the hair-raising escapades, the alien cities, the amazing creatures, the light of other suns....

And, to the Vizier: "Do I own a whisperlyre?"

Twenty-One

The Soldier, the Bard, and the Whore

... the dream ...

... rock striking child's head ... crying, crying ... but the child ... is it me? ... or am I watching?

His eyes were trying to open now but he didn't want them to. He tried to squeeze them tighter. But something was forcing them.

... rock striking ...

He was numb. He couldn't move his limbs at all. But his eyes ... they blinked. They were crusted, but he couldn't move his hand to rub his eyelids. No.

Now he could. Slowly, slowly, as though emerging from —

"Stasis."

A familiar voice.

"Mikkálu!" Rage shook his mind, but his body would not rage along with it. Instead the rage went inward. Like bottling up a hurricane.

"You'll come to soon," Mikkálu said. The boy was standing in front of him.

Standing in a corridor, with frozen children on either side, stretching into darkness as far as the eye could see. The children in single file. The corridor — a little curved — like a tunnel — a cavern. The walls, segmented, as though they were inside a metallic annelid.

The only light came from Mikkálu himself. His eyes were projecting a pool of cold blue light.

"Not something the planetbound get to see that often," Mikkálu said. "They think — a childsoldier's eyes, they only spit out killing lines of laser light. But there are other settings. They are a marvel of the thinkhives' inventiveness. My eyes can give off light … I can even cook a piece of meat with them. And make it precisely medium rare. In a millisecond."

"You killed my father! You snatched away my brother!"

Sajit could not feel Tijas at all; the bond had been cut off as soon as he was sucked into the belly of the delphinoid.

... *rock striking* ...

"You more than took him away. I can't even feel him."

"Ah.   The notorious doppling psychic link. Studied by scientists, explained by no one. *Abomination!*"

Sajit winced.

"I know. I don't know how much it hurts. It's not in my worldview to have a psychic link with anyone. But then ... I grew up in that whorehouse you call a temple, and I was in love with the goddess."

"Not any more?" Sajit said.

"The next time we see this world again — if we live through a war or two — a long time will have passed. This is time dilation. See all those other kids? They'll wake up, a second after they were sucked up the shaft, and only the powers of powers will now how much realtime has gone by. Forget Urna. Forget Alykh. Forget it all, Sajitteh."

"Don't call me by my child-name."

"Oh ... Sajitteh ... you don't know it yet, but I am your only friend on this ship. I'm the only one who understands even a scintilla of what's in your brain."

"Why would you be my friend? Why am I not in stasis anyway?"

"I didn't mean to kill him," Mikkálu said. "You know that." For a moment he seemed strangely vulnerable. "And you have done something bad to me, too, though you don't realize it. Because of the ruckus you and your twin created, I'm no longer the Child Collector's favorite equerry. I'm off the roster. And guess what my last order was? To fetch *you.*"

"Me?"

"You're the new favorite now. I think it really excites him, you know, *down there,* to think he has all this power over someone of royal blood. Someone they went through *such* trouble to conceal. Well, I wish you all joy of your newfound status."

"But what do I have to do?"

"Anything he tells you. And don't think your blue blood can fend off a beating. Or even a rape."

"Rape?"

"You seem very ignorant, Sajitteh, or else you've lived a sheltered life. Rape is like making love, except you do it with hate. Sound familiar? Maybe you've experimented with your twin? Another perquisite of the psychic link?"

But Sajit was thinking of the space between spaces. How he and Tijas had melded into one attenuated entity, in a place without dimensions. He ached. "I don't care what becomes of me now," he said.

"I daresay you will avoid ill treatment," Mikkálu said, "as I always do. With my attitude. He likes attitude. His corpse lovers never give him any."

It was then than Sajit saw a bruise on Mikkálu's arm, and he knew there was pain behind his bluster. *My mother loved him — believed he'd do anything for her, including killing one of* me, he thought.

"I won't be having so many privileges anymore," Mikkálu said. "I might need your help."

Sajit put out his hand and the boys touched fingertips. "All right," he said. "Take me to see him."
***

A room in Alykh: candied, rosy light, lush, cushiony music of shimmerviols, a bedfloat. The woman who was once a goddess was not cloaked in shadow. She wore an extravagant kaleidofur loosely wrapped, like a blanket, which blinked in and out with her heartbeat. She wore a hairpiece fashioned from arachnid silk, a living spiderweb that wove and unwove itself in the air around her.

Lang viHurek had made a deal after all. The tourist board would reconstruct the temple as a sensuality theme park, and the goddess would be chair of the advisory board.

In a tennight she and her former acolytes had taken over a row of shophouses in the whores' district of Aírang. The word was already getting out that the practitioners of this establishment had skilled that were, literally, of mythic proportions. Sex rituals of a dead planet. The temple would be for fooling *dorezdas;* this alley would be the real thing.

The door sang out, "A client."

"Come!" she said, with a cunningly modulated half-laugh in her voice.

There was an old man in the doorway, dressed in the manner of Urna — this, already, was beginning to seem quaint. The old man had a baby in his arms, and a battered whisperlyre hung about his waist.

"I am —"

"Arbát," said Éluma. "I try to remember all our former congregation."

Arbát said, "I've done many terrible things, goddess. And so have you."

"Who is the child?" But she knew already.

"Look at him. Do you feel *abomination?* Does your blood curdle, do you want to hurl stones?"

Éluma said, "Yes. I do feel ... a twinge of horror." *Harám, harám,* her mind cried out, *and yet —*

"I took the doppling kit from the ruined home of Ina desAreon. There was enough of a charge left, enough DNA left on this old whisperlyre to unlock it, to seed it. There may be more than one charge left, in fact. The copy may be imperfect. I cannot tell. They were only designed to function once. Yet I could not resist, goddess."

"I've failed as a goddess, and I've failed as a mother," Éluma said.

"But now there's a chance to start over. Hold him. Look into his eyes."

The old musician placed the child in the crook of her arm. The child's eyes opened and he gurgled. His eyes ... *my eyes*, she thought.

"Don't you see, Éluma-without-a-Clan? This is a new world. We are other people now, though we wear the same flesh and blood. We can begin again. And why not begin by naming him?"

"Jatis," she said without hesitation.

"Look! Is the baby smiling?"

***

There were no displacement plates in the tunnels and it was a long trudge — perhaps two klomets — to get to an antique door that opened by applying physical pressure to a lever, and which swung open like the lid of a box.

On the other side, there were the normal cabins, displacement plates, holosculpt environments. But no virtual windows.

Looking on the overcosm drives men mad ... Sajit knew this well ... it was something every child knows.

"Quick, come," Mikkálu said. He took Sajit's hand and lead him through more plates —

More cabins of frozen people — childsoldiers, accountants, chefs, jugglers, carelessly stacked like toys, on shelves, waiting to come to life —

And finally the Child Collector's chamber.

It was a kind of inferno. The floor was strewn with servocorpses, maimed, decapitated, tortured, some simulating death (though they were dead anyway), others groaning, clawing their way around the room. And there was Gharém, whom Sajit had last seen decked in a ceremonial uniform. Now he was naked and in the throes of —

Sajit remembered spying on Arbát.

Bursting the milkpod.

"My Lord," Mikkálu said, ignoring the ghastly spectacle, "I've brought you Sajit-without-a-Clan, as you ordered."

The Child Collector stood, sweaty and disheveled, and and turned a beady gaze on Sajit. Meanwhile, Mikkálu was setting the chamber to order, switching off the corpses and putting them away in a closet that irised open in the wall, restoring the room to a more formal environment, with a starscape and dragon-shaped nebulae.

"So you're my new equerry," said Kyar Garém.

"I don't even know what an equerry is, sir," Sajit said.

"It's an Old Earth position. Something to do with horses."

"Horses?"

"They look like hippopters, but without wings. Before there were starships, people rode them. How they rode horses them to the stars, I know not. It is a myth — like the homeworld of the heart itself."

Gharém summoned a chairfloat and sat cross-legged in the air.

"Master Gharém," Mikkálu said, "shall I leave you to torment your new plaything?"

Gharém made to slap the boy's face, and Mikkálu had genuine terror in his eyes, for just a second, before reverting to his cocky self.

"You'd never, Lord." he said. "Why, you know I could slice off your hand with a single glance."

"As well you could, Mikkálu. But you won't. You've been well programmed. You couldn't resist my authority no matter how hard you tried. This other one, on the other hand...."

"Don't harm him," Mikkálu said. "This one, the Inquestors themselves are looking out for."

"Indeed. You have, perhaps, a great destiny, Sajit-without-a-Clan. But to reach it, you must first pass through the fire. It is as they say in the song — the one about the million boys who dream."

"Yes, Lord Gharém," Sajit said.

"But first, a gift."

Even Mikkálu gasped. The Child Collector, it seemed, did not *give* anyone anything.

He hopped off the chairfloat and waddled over to the closet which parted a little at his subvoked command; he reached in a pulled out a whisperlyre. "It is a rustic thing," he said, "which I acquired on ... some world we wiped out. The tree it was carved from is of a species that is no more. Its whispers are the sighs of worlds *fallen beyond* forever."

He tossed the whisperlyre over. When Sajit's fingers touched the dead wood he could feel it living. It had a soul. It had been waiting since its world's destruction for the touch that would give life to all it remembered. Already it had started to whisper, sussuration of sympathetic strings tuning itself to the vibrations of his hands, his heart.

The Child Collector climbed back on the chairfloat. "Now, Mikkálu," he said, "I've demoted you to a common dogsbody. And for the mess you made of my collection, I should probably have beaten you, although we are far too refined to *actually* beat people, are we not?"

"The threat is bad enough, Master Gharém," said Mikkálu with a mock groan. Yet Sajit could tell that the threat was not entirely empty.

"So you shall not have the privilege of attending me when I rest," said Gharém. "Instead, I shall have ... *Sajit* ... sing me to sleep. I have been told that the whole universe will know his songs one day. Well,

I'm going to the first. And if his songs do not please me, perhaps … the universe will *not* know them."

And he laughed — the laughter of evil villains — from which Sajit realized that this was a vulnerable and insecure old man after all. Like Arbát. And not as evil as he himself would have wanted to appear.

"Well now, my Princeling-without-a-Planet, let me hear about loss, about desire, and about longing for that which can never come," said the Child Collector, "so that my own pain can be stilled a little. And you, Mikállu, you miscreant — don't come back unless you are summoned."

All right. Sajit told himself. "Since you spoke of it, Lord Gharém, I'll sing the song called *Asheveraín*, a song about the Homeworld of the Heart.

He thought of his two mothers and his two fathers. Dead, perhaps. Or stranded in a world they could never return to. His sisters. He didn't even know if they had survived the people bins' planetfall. Guilt and sadness came all at once. He clenched back his tears.

Tijas! If I could only summon you … even a shadow's shadow … for though we inhabit separate flesh, we are one person.

He began to weep, and as his tears dripped on the strings of the whisperlyre their whispering became a shimmering, fluctuating harmony …

***

... and Tijas went to the forest beside the village with the clearing of singing moons, because he knew it would remind him of Sajit.

He went alone. As Sajit had.

But it was not the same, because when Sajit used to go there, there was no Tijas. And when Tijas came it was not as some village boy dreaming of stars and moons, but as Princeling able to buy them.

And though he walked into the clearing alone, a small group of attendants stood just out of reach and out of sight. And after a moment in the clearing, he told himself, he would go back to his courtiers. And plan his voyage.

That was how it had been when the last Princeling of Urna came to the clearing, hoping to catch a glimpse of his son.

Three of the moons were full. It was a clear night, and chill; the perfect time to imagine the singing of the moons.

Tijas had a whisperlyre with him; they had found one somewhere in the palace, in the museum collections which had somehow remained intact.

It was a pristine instrument. He did not know what others remained in the museum, but he would restore them all one day. And create an army of bards.

He tuned the whisperlyre beneath a tree.

What did the moons say?

You are not who you think you are.

That was what they had told Sajit ... a memory whose edge he had touched, in the space between spaces.

He sounded a note, the note that is called *dha,* which sometimes called *thunder.* On this whisperlyre *dha* was the fundamental tone and when he touched it, the tree itself trembled and he felt the sympathetic vibration deep inside himself.

He sang:

Pu eyáh chítarans hyemadh?
Where is the homeworld of the heart?

A question asked a million times by a million poets of the Dispersal of Man.

Sajit! he cried out in his mind. *Up there, somewhere, perhaps in stasis, silenced by the space between spaces.*

Shenom na chítarans hyemadhá
We yearn for the heart's homeworld ...

It was an ancient song that children know. A melody so simple a beginner can strum it, yet so subtle that only a great artist can do it justice.

***

Sajit sang:

am plánzhet ka dhand-erúden
We wept for the dead Earth ...

and saw that Gharém was already asleep on his chairfloat, and snoring a little. The room, cleared of corpses, was no longer a brothel of the dead.

But he was not singing for anyone who claimed to own him.

He was singing to Tijas.

Or rather, *with* Tijas.

For though time and space are relative, there is synchronicity in souls, and in the spaces between spaces all points in spacetime are adjacent.

And so, for a second that seemed to last forever — he felt his twin, and knew his twin felt *him*.

Tijas! he cried out.   And heard his doppling's answer even as he cried out: *Sajit!*

It lasted only a moment after all.

But the moment had been long enough for him to realize ...

Tijas! There's another —
***

—one in here with us, Tijas answered.
***

"Look! Is the baby smiling?"

CHRONICLES OF THE HIGH INQUEST
THE SIXTH VOLUME

Stillness in Starlight

by S.P. Somtow

Úran brendéh!
Áther dhandáh!
Niká mi zeranýmuu
Dhanati neveláh !

Má eih airánduteh,
Akosáis ke hokhté
Darluktá akinteh!

The sky is burning!
The sun is dying!
My planet chokes
On the smoke of death!

But oh my beloved
Could you but hear
The stillness in starlight!

— from the Songs of Sajit

Prologue
Lost in a Labyrinth of Timelines

When an Inquestor dreams, does reality condense out of the chaos of his fleeting visions?

For Ton Elloran n'Taanyel Tath was dreaming.

A hearse drawn by pteratygers ... the velvet light of Uran s'Varek, a million suns softened by a thousand klomets of atmosphere ... an old man and a young woman, watching.

When your life is the very substance of men's mythology, what is truth?

A rainbow castle disintegrating in a bright blue sky.

When the timeline of your existence pierces and spirals and slices through the timeline of history, what is *your* history?

A planet made of dust. And out of the dust, a woman.

If a deeper truth underlies your truth, how many layers deep must you dive to discover the truth of all truths?

***

Sajit! So many memories, so many non-memories, so much hearsay, so many truths and half-truths, all contradictions, all fleeting.

I name you to the clan of Shen.

That really happened.   Elloran could cast his memory back a century of subjective time, millennia of time elapsed through time dilation, to when two children stood before an old man on a hoverthrone and ripped apart his painstakingly crafted false utopia.

I was a child, Elloran thought, *yet more than a child because I was already an Inquestor. An Inquestor who does not weep. An Inquestor who, from compassion, must learn pitilessness.*

It really happened.   They were two children crossing a wasteland disguised as a paradise, riding the pteratyger up to the rainbow palace … and for the duration not Inquestor and childsoldier, not near-god and lowest of peons, but just two people.…

Elloran remembered first hearing Sajit's song, a song, the boy said, that had been taught him by some drifter who stole him and abandoned him in the firesnows of Ont —

Shenom na chítarans hyemadhá
… Z'púrreh y'Enguestren tinjéh …

We long for the heart's homeworld

... Where the Inquestor touches the beggar child....

But it was not like that. Not for the two of them. For a moment, they had been truly equal. It felt that way. Only afterwards, when paradise disintegrated, when the utopia had truly been hunted and killed, did they move into the roles of master and servant. And it had happened with that one sentence:

I name you to the clan of Shen.

One tiny display of power. Not an unwanted display, for it was what Sajit had dreamed for all his tender life. But it was a moment that ended equality for ever.

Had they been lovers, as was whispered behind his back at countless games of *makrúgh,* as was sung openly in taverns and streets by half-gipfer bards and bad poets drunk on dreamstuff?

Perhaps, except that an Inquestor does not *love.* An Inquestor may take anything he wishes. There is never any question, never any free will, on the part of the one he takes from.

Yet —

All these tellings. Of little green memory worms connecting the mind to generations of history. Of princelings and goddesses, of arduous training in the art of song, of civilizations colliding ... was it true, after all, that the two were so unequal?

Was the Sajit he first met not, after all, an abandoned slum child, abused and beaten and sucked into childsoldiery at random, a piece of galactic refuse washed up at the young Inquestor's feet? Did he, even then, have millennial memories of kingship, and a thinkhive-sized repertoire of ancient music? It was not the Sajit he remembered.

Unless the Sajit he first met was a Sajit who had *chosen* to forget....

***

On a dull world with a sleepy starport and a single village, a world that no longer even had a name ... an Inquestor had come.

He had come to remember, to affirm. But each fact to be affirmed shifted in the observation, like a subatomic particle.

In a few sleeps Ton Elloran had learned from the Rememberer Tash Toléon that the Sajit he knew was not altogether Sajit.

The Sajit he had known all his life, the Sajit whose funeral he witnessed against the backdrop of Shentrazjit, the Singing City ... could not also be buried in two places ... but he was.

The Sajit that grew up in a slum could not have been the Sajit who had been the designated heir of a Princeling ... but he was.

There were *two* Sajits.

Perhaps, it seemed, even *three*.

***

Varezhdur, the starfaring wonderland, still orbited the nameless world that had once been Alykh, the pleasure planet … and before that Urna, a backworld with quaint traditions.

Yet Ton Elloran n'Taanyel Tath did not want to return there. He was still sitting in a shabby room in a museum unvisited in generations, in a village called Sajittang on the unnamed world, trying to piece together the true nature of a man he had once loved.

Was *love* even the right word? As the High Inquest moved inexorably into decline, its moved to the music and imagery of Sajit the poet, the musician, the one beloved by the most beloved of Inquestors. All educated people knew a snatch or two of a melody, some curious, characteristic melisma, some turn of phrase, some metaphor … Sajit's was the voice of the Inquest's fall.

***

As Tash Toléon observed him warily (for even an Inquestor fast asleep is to be feared) Ton Elloran lay on an cushion of force; a light amnio-rain sprinkled from an unseen source. In his arms he cradled a jangling ard discordant whisperlyre.

Does an Inquestor truly dream at all, or are his dreams but a higher reality?

Sajitteh!

A galaxy of dust had swirled in the throneroom of Varezhdur.

Sajitteh!

Elloran woke, murmuring Sajit's child-name.

"Do you want to hear more, hokh'Ton?" the Rememberer asked. "Because now there is a branching off of the tale. There may be gaps, even parts of the story not Remembered at all. And that is disturbing to me, a member of the Clan of Tash, who live only for the sake of Remembrance."

"Can you tell me nothing?"

"I can, my Lord. As the generations passed and we waited for your coming, more was gleaned about the Sajits. But I cannot say if the stories passed through many mouths or one. As for *objective* truth —"

"Perhaps unknowable. But, Toléon, I would at least know *my* truth."

Sajitteh! The light inside the galaxy of dust!

"At times, hokh'Ton, what I tell you may seem to come more from the mind of a storyteller than a mnemonicist, and some parts may be fragmentary and confused, yet I promise you a shining truth in every fragment, no matter how jagged or murky it may seem. Trust me, Lord Inquestor. Remember that my whole life, and that of many generations of rememberers before me, has been lived to bring you these glittering nuggets of perception."

"I will listen, Toléon. And yet—"

***

Suddenly he could stay there no longer. The journey without an ending in sight, the splitting of the timelines ... *I need to sit in a familiar place.* Elloran summoned his floater.

"I'll return," he told Toléon. "I don't know when. But I will return; I must." For now, the weight of memory was too oppressive.

He summoned his floater in minutes he was in Varezhdur once more.

Varezhdur! All spires and curlicues and spirals and curves, cushioned in the pearly glow of its own corona!

The ultimate in elegance, each room a marvel, with simple, sweeping lines. Rooms carpeted with living shimmerfur, flowing soft pink against dark blue, rooms with floors and walls of wafer-thin calliliths, vast rooms with a single holosculpt as centerpiece.

In one the great halls, a game of *makrúgh* was proceeding, with half a dozen Inquestors on hoverthrones, darting about, scheming, insinuating, dissembling, weaving tapestries of casuistry on looms of doublespeak, sipping fresh blood from the wounds of a crucified narwhal.   Elloran had not even known such a game was going on in Varezhdur; he himself had long lost interest in such things.

***

Varezhdur is a palace, a city, and more than a city. No resident could know every room, every corridor, let alone its Lord.   There were those who lived out their lives in Varezhdur without even knowing that it could fly to any place in the Dispersal of Man, who did not even know that Varezhdur was not the universe.

Many who lived there had probably never set eyes on the Inquestor who was starting to be called, with a tremulous affection, *hokh'Airándut,* the High Beloved.

There was one now, perhaps, hurrying down a passageway, a hood drawn over his face for fear of being seen in such an exalted sector of the palace.

"Stop," Elloran said and the man looked as though he were going to faint.   However, he performed the prostration with grace.   Elloran supposed that, growing up as he has in Varezhdur, the etiquette must have been drilled into him since childhood.   "Let me see your face."

"Hokh'Ton!" Eyes of a frightened rodent.

"What do you do here?"

"I'm only a scullery drudge," said the man.   "I'm … I'm extremely lowly.   I was sent to fetch frozen gruyesh chips from one of the larder levels. I must have subvoked a wrong command." He looked back down at the floor immediately, and pulled his hood tighter; his face was shadowed once again. "I shouldn't be in such an area, reserved for the Exalted."

"On the contrary," Elloran said, laughing, "you're just the person I want to talk to. Do you have a name?"

"I am Taraq-without-a-clan, hokh'Ton."

"I want to see where you live."

"That would be ..." Taraq looked away.

"You were going to say embarrassing, or shameful," Elloran said. "Instead say that it is an honor. Get up off the floor, old man, you'll fracture your knees."

The man began to shuffle toward a side corridor which narrowed and appeared to be descending on a steep incline. This part of the palace, it seemed, was not so carefully gravity-controlled. Presently Elloran encountered something even more antiquarian — *steps*. A spiral staircase than went down and down and down. He knew what they were, of course, staircases were common enough as a *motif* in elegant décor. But to actually use them as means of travel. *Quaint*, he thought, *and in my own palace.*

"We do not use displacement?"

"Oh, no, hokh'Ton. The plates on the lower levels are just two to a linear klomet. This is faster, and better exercise."

They had climbed down about ten levels, judging each level to be twice a human's height. A dark fragrance seeped into the stairwell.

They stood on a metal landing; looking below Elloran could see that the stairwell stretched beyond his line of sight. A door irised and they stepped into a cramped hallway that opened into a kitchen. People were scurrying about with loaves and amphoras and hovertrays and pots from which billowed the heavy aroma he had smelled outside.

Somewhere in the distance, there came the sound of a *klazmurah*, people clapping, a wailing shalmó and the strumming of a tribal kithara.

A rotund woman appeared. "Where's my gruyesh?"

"I got ... delayed, Auntie."

"You silly man!" She suddenly noticed the Inquestor, and almost tripped over herself to perform a proper prostration. Around them, it suddenly got quiet, and cooks and lackeys were abruptly all face down on the floor, having done the prostration en masse, as though to pulse of a timing-stick.

"No ceremony, please," Elloran said. "I wish to—"

The woman cackled a little. "Have you come to count all the people you own?"

"I do not own you," Elloran said.

"Indeed, hokh'Ton. We all know you have an aversion to servocorpses. Everyone knows the story of the Rainbow King. Sit, *hokh'Airándut,* and I'll bring you a posset. Up, up, on your feet, children," she said to the others, who slowly arose and started bustling about, "Our Inquestor isn't one of the arrogant ones, you know."

She proffered a chair — a physical chair of wood, he noted, not a cunning bending of space and lines of force.

It was at that moment that Elloran recognized the song that was coming from the other room. The words were blunted and in the lowspeech, but the melody, crudely underscored with a monotonous seven-beat cycle, was still recognizable....

Vi shena nar chrtas himaith
U ater tezh' eruda —

"We long for the heart's homeworld," the Inquestor murmured, translating the words into the Highspeech. "But that is Sajit's song."

"Hokh'Ton, Shen Sajit himself taught it to us."

"You *knew* him?" How could such a thing be possible? They were shortlivers, and Sajit ... had lived in the timespan of Inquestors.

"Why, when he was a boy, he often scrounged for scraps in this very kitchen."

"Scraps?" Surely Sajit had been well fed enough, could ask for anything to eat without—

"He was a sweet boy.   He missed his mother, really.   Not saying there's anything wrong with the fine viands we serve up there, mind you.   What a love! Why, I'd give him a chocolate bun, and he'd kiss me on the cheek. His mother hated him, you know."

"You speak so casually of the Inquestor's bard?"

"Powers of powers, hokh'Ton.   You're so high above us.   But he loved *you*, Inquestor.   And you never could see how much. You're so high above us. You're not capable of it."

"But I too—" Elloran began.

"You people don't always know everything.   The ones on the planets can worship and prostrate … in your house, we know where you fart."

Elloran laughed. A throaty, full, infectious laugh, for it overcame the others' diffidence.   *Why have I waited so long to know anything about the denizens of my own palace? When* Sajit *clearly knew them?*

"Come," said the woman called "Auntie".   "It is my granddaughter's wedding."

***

Another hallway and then—

A room transformed into a village, by walls that had projected rich holosculpts— here a fountain, there a modest temple, here a square with simple flagstones, and a pale, large, lonely moon, as described in myths of Old Earth. The *klazmurah* of seven musicians sat in a gazebo. No sophisticated courtly instruments, but a twanging kithara and a shalmó, and a rhythm section made from cooking-jars.

Men and women were clapping and dancing, dance of abandonment with the extra kick on the seventh beat causing much merriment, waving fire-tinged neckerchiefs … for all the world as though they were reenacting some ancient ritual. Then came a processional, the bride on a palanquin, veiled in red; the groom on another, veiled in blue; for neither had ever set eyes on the other; so vast was Varezhdur, it could house multiple colonies of differing languages and homeworlds.

"This is how they get married on your homeworld, Auntie?" Elloran asked the woman. She was probably young enough to be his granddaughter, of course. But he did not yet know her name.

People were coming up to congratulate her; she was nodding and and smiling. "Why, Hokh'Ton," she said. "Varezhdur is my homeworld. I actually *could* be your auntie, for our palace has gone everywhere that you went, and any time dilation you gods experienced, we did too. Some here, I think, we taken from their worlds, whether bought or invited; I was born here, when the foundations of Varezhdur had been laid, before you, hokh'Ton, acquired it and grew it to this flying wonder."

And Elloran wondered that even now there were things he took for granted ... that when his ship rode the delphinoid currents of the overcosm, an entire staff was being dragged along with it, and losing their families and their past in the process—it was something Inquestors never even considered. It was not something ever spoken of in the teachings of the High Compassion. It was simply a given.

Did this woman have an "auntie" she might have buried two centuries ago?

He was happier than ever to be leaving all this behind.

With a clash of gongs, the bride and groom unveiled themselves. The girl shrieked — but surely not from displeasure, for the groom was handsome.

And then, all at once—

The entire room, this entire village packed into a chamber set in a holosculpted world, hundreds of men, women and children fell to their knees. Their gaze all turned downward ... yet all were also looking up, in adoration, at the High Beloved.

And they all started to sing the Inquestral Anthem.

I, a slave, a chattel, a nothing
  throw down before you all my heart
  my thoughts, the works of my hands
  O you who bask in the High Compassion....

How many times had Ton Elloran heard those
words?   Heard them thundering from a sky whose
suns were eclipsed by a million childsoldiers whirling
in their deadly hoverdisks?

What could induce more awe, more terror, more
savage beauty than a million young lives offering to
throw their very existences away on some mission of
the High Compassion?   Yet Elloran had become
inured to the spectacle.

This was different.   The woman *knew* Sajit ... she,
too, had loved him.   Perhaps genuinely, for an
Inquestor cannot love.

Here, he was so moved that unwittingly, he started
to do the unthinkable.   No, they could not see him
weep.   Quickly he backed away, reached behind to
touch the wall, to find a displacement stud that only
he could activate—

And subvocalized a single word, *Retrograde.*

The thinkhive of Varezhdur brought him to where
he had been not long before, in the corridor, just
before he had run into Taraq.   As soon has he was
gone, he lost control; warm tears spurted.   His
shimmercloak rustled; it *knew* that its master was in

an impossible emotional state; a the human-sized single-cell organism that melded with its Inquestor's consciousness for life, and knew his feelings better than he did himself. Quickly it moved to mask Elloran's face, to suck his lachrymal secretions into itself, for that was how it fed.

Poor cloak! Elloran thought. *So much emotion may cause it to sicken and wilt away.*

The cloak shifted again. Someone was there.
***

She wore her shimmercloak almost transparently, while her long, dark hair wrapped itself around her breasts. She had a clear laugh which made her seem young; she had kept the shape of an adolescent, and had bleached her skin to an unnatural white, but Elloran could see in her eyes how she had aged. It was Ton Siriss, his protégée, his designated successor.

"Sirissheh," he said softly. "I didn't know there was *makrúgh* in Varezhdur today."

"We were so deeply involved, Loreh," she said, and her use of his child-name was both playful and ironic, "that no one noticed the palace had entered the overcosm, and has been in orbit around a strange world for many sleeps."

"Did it change anything? He did not tell her that he had recently learned that *makrúgh* can misfire. It would not help to tell her this. An Inquestor must *never* be wrong. An Inquestor must be the very core of certitude. Or all collapses.

"No it did not, Ton Elloran n'Taanyel Tath," she said more formally. "Seven worlds are up for grabs. I tell you this because you yourself are abstaining from the game. Otherwise I wouldn't of course. What planet is this?"

"It's Shen Sajit's burial place. Or so say the legends."

"That makes no sense, Loreh," she said. "You and I were at his funeral. He is—"

"Among the srinjids, on Uran s'Varek; he is the grain of sand around which the perfect symphony was formed. Yes, yes. I was there. Yet, it seems, he is here, too."

"Oh, Loreh, you are obsessed. When will you let go? You held him close, it is true. You loved the same woman, and you loved each other more. *Evendek ma Enguester eís, evendek fáh, evendek seréh.*"

"True. But this is not denying my nature. This is about something factual. He *does* lie in both places. And maybe others."

"Not true, Elloran. Even a clone is not a true copy."

"We know that ... but do *they?*"

"Loreh ... be careful. I say this because I am the closest thing to a daughter that you've ever had ... that you *could* have, as reproduction is forbidden to us. You haven't come to terms with it. Do you remember the things you said to me that day on Uran s'Varek?"

I don't need a Rememberer for that, he thought. *It's burned into remembrance.* "I gave you this palace," he said. "I told you I was going to … turn to simpler pursuits."

"And when were you actually going to hand it over, Ton Elloran n'Taanyel Tath? Not that I would ever hurry you, of course. What is a century or two? Yet maybe we don't have a century or two. Did you not tell me, *The Inquest falls?* Is there any evidence of this? Where is the war of whispershadows?"

"Soon," Elloran said. "Perhaps, it has already fallen. It depends, I think, on where you stand … in time, in space, in your perception of the universe."

"I've got seven devious minds in the gaming-chamber that don't believe it has fallen … or will ever fall. They cannot imagine it."

"Then you'd better go in there and save a few planets," Elloran said. "Run along, my dear."

Ton Siriss laughed. "You've been crying," she said. "But don't worry. I'm the only person who could possibly notice."

***

He had her brought to the room with the galaxy of dust. It was not *the* galaxy of dust … he had destroyed that one a few times, sometimes in a rage, sometimes because the memory was too bitter. But Varezhdur's thinkhive was always a step ahead; and it could replicate the dust-sculpture to the molecule.

She entered and began to prostrate herself, but he stopped her.

"I didn't bring you here to fawn," he told her. "I want to learn from you."

She came closer then, looked up, looked him in the eye. "Even when you quarrelled," she said, "he always believed in your goodness."

"What is your name?" he said.

"Auntie," she said.

"But you have a birth name...."

"I have forgotten it," she said.

"You have some tradition," he said, "perhaps, of never revealing your true name to those outside your immediate circle."

"Nothing so arcane," she said. "Look, I brought you a fresh-baked loaf of *peftifesht*."

He ordered a chairfloat for her, but she preferred the floor; she was a little stumped when it moulded itself to her body, but she settled in. And so he began.

He told her about Sajittang. About the Rememberer, about the Princeling of Urna, about the doppling kit, about the clashing of the two civilizations in a mismatched *makrúgh*. He told her about the Child Collector, and about the Goddess of Love who had become a whore.

He told her about the boy so like and so unlike the childsoldier he had met so long ago, who had grown up alongside him, who had moved into Varezhdur with him, whose music had woven itself into every moment of his life, waking and sleeping.

"The boy Tash Toléon described was Sajit in every way—he looked like him, spoke like him, thought like him. But there was ... a wrongness. Where was the child of the slums, taught to sing by a stranger, so innocent yet so knowing of the darkness in the human soul?"

"You've come to the right woman," said Auntie. "I know, you will have to go back to the surface and see your Rememberer again. But if you want to know about that skinny little boy ... the scruffy boy who grew up fleecing the *dorezdas* in the back streets of the City of Love ... the boy whose mother treated him like a dirty secret ... then you must ask me. Because I *knew* that very boy. He talked to me. Right in my kitchen. It came tumbling from his lips, jumbled and sometimes mixed with tears. It wasn't an accident that you bumped into our Taraq, hokh'Ton. I sent him to find you."

And she began to tell him a different story. And she, too, was a kind of Rememberer. Though her diction was unpolished, her tale was as vivid as a trained clansman of Tash. And so it was that Elloran began to understand the life of the second doppling, the one named Jatis.

One
City of Love, City of Shame

Aírang, the city woven from rainbows, city of a million colored lights, city of beauty, city of whores, city where everything is for sale, city where everything is free for the asking; Aírang, capital city of the pleasure world called Alykh, the world that shifts from world to world, the world that doesn't stay put, the world that can never remain the world for long because it is too valuable a prize in the Inquestral game of *makrúgh* ... Aírang, called the City of Love.

Though *love* in Aírang can be a dirty word.

I do this because I love you.

When the boy's mother spat it out, her eyes envenomed by an unknown emotion, he couldn't help himself. Tears welled up. It wasn't so much the slap as the shame.

"Go!" she screamed after him. "It's time to call the Old Man anyway ... the one who left you on my doorstep." He could hear her crying now, and he thought to himself, *No. I won't go back. I won't comfort her.*

He ran outside, almost forgetting to dissolve the door.

Dorezdas lined the street, plating up out of the mass-displacement-transit-plate one and two at a time, clutching their bags of gipfers or twiddling their credit-thumbs, brazen or hiding their faces under layers of clingfire, strutting or sneaking, the nightly clientele of Dromek Vornã, the alley of the whores.

Sobbing, he darted between the clients. No one saw him. He turned a corner, took a tunnel and ended up two displacements later at the edge of a lake.

It was evening and the red sun of Alykh made the trees cast shadows, a deeper purple even than the leaves, and overhead two loons circled, glowing and screeching. Behind the loons, moons danced.

He was a small boy like a lot of small boys growing up in the slums of the city ... growing up among prostitutes with a single mother who smiled all day long for strangers and came back up to the room too tired to talk to her child ... a mother who, he knew in his heart, despite her insistence ... a mother who *hated* him. He was hungry. He felt completely alone.

He sat at the edge of the lake and cried until long past sunset. But in the City of Love the night is brighter than the day. Phallus-shaped fireworks burst over the lake. The moons themselves moved in a lazy minuet, first Arrisát and Káruval and then the others, and a flock of moonlets behind them.

He had cried himself into kind of stupor. He was in a state where he was almost outside himself. He knew what was going to happen next ... it always happened, when he found himself in such a paroxysm ... suddenly he found himself *somewhere else.*

He saw stars.

Not the night sky over Aírang. That was a sky luminous and chaotic, with stars and moons and moonlets and shards of people bins and shuttles streaking back and forth from the starport.

The stars he saw were bright and completely still.

And they were set in a tapestry blacker than any darkweaving.

He'd heard once that when you leave the atmosphere, the stars no longer twinkle. He could imagine such a thing: an infinity of points of unwavering light. *But I'm not imagining this,* he thought. *I'm seeing this for real.*

And not through another person's eyes. It's me *who is seeing this, and it's* now *that it's happening.*

When the boy closed his eyes the image was still there.

They were uncountable, and brighter than they could possibly be in any night of Aírang. In the utter stillness of this starlight, the boy felt … *longing.*

Someone sees me.

In his rundown apartment on Dromek Vornã, no one saw him at all, not even his mother. He didn't know why she hated him. She slapped him from time to time, but he didn't think she meant to hurt him … or to hate him, for that matter. There were just things he didn't know. Maybe to do with the Old Man. On Vornã mothers warned their children of "old men" all the time, but this was different.

The boy sat up.

I guess I have to go back now, he thought.

But as he pulled himself up from the purple grass he felt a hand on his shoulder. And when he whipped around it was the very thing his mother had used to threaten him. It was an old man. No — it was *the* Old Man. He just knew it.

"You've been crying," the Old Man said.

"What business is it of yours? Leave me alone," the boy said. As any child would say to a stranger who put a gnarled hand on his shoulder. The boy shook himself a bit, pulled his hemáti tighter about his shoulder, as the night had become suddenly chilly.

The Old Man wasn't dressed like someone from this world. But he didn't seem like a *dorezda,* either. He was wore a white cloak over an undergarment woven from darkness. He had a wispy beard and a crooked nose. He cheeks and forehead were weathered, and had not even covered his face with a cosmetic epiderm as any decent Airángi would do before leaving the house.

He was frightening and yet ... familiar.

"Do you ever sing?" the Old Man said.

"Of course not," the boy said, startled. "Singing is for fine palaces ... or two-gipfer whores. But I'll sing for two gipfers," he added, thinking he might buy himself some zul.

The Old Man laughed. "I'd pay it," he said.

"All right then," the boy said. He started to pose, the way he'd seen street performers do, thrusting his hand in the air and taking a deep breath.

"No, no, not here. There's a place."

"Oh, no, you don't," said the boy.

He has an accent, he realized suddenly. *The same accent my mother has. People who talk that way are ... somehow like us,* he thought.

"Oh come. You know very well I'm not one of the 'those' old men, Jatis—"

"My name!"

He has my mother's accent and he knows my name.

The chill was bone-deep, and it wasn't just the wind. "You're *the* Old Man," Jatis said. "The one who abandoned me in the street of the whores, the one who's coming to take me back if I'm a bad boy."

"I am at that."

The Old Man shook his head.

"Give me the two gipfers, then," said Jatis. "I want to buy something to eat. I'll even sing something."

"I'll take you to eat something."

"No! You don't get to take me away for two gipfers!"

"Would you like to visit another world?"

"No!"

"We'll be back in an hour."

"You're a lying old man. Go fuck a servocorpse."

"Oh, I will, I will, Jatis, but not today. Today I will take to have a bowl of the finest chocolate in the galaxy, melted and melded with mildly fermented gruyesh and topped with a candied beetle drowning in a dreamberry coulis. And *then* you will sing."

"What's chocolate?" Jatis said.

***

A pathway. Two displacements. A wall.

An antique wall, in fact, made of real material, not holosculpted force. You could tell by the smell.

It was high enough that Jatis could not see over the top. It was a wall made from reddish blocks of baked earth, the crannies filled with wild rosellas, strings and strings of them, the petals fluttering like pale snow.

Vines grew in profusion, too. They overhung the wall. The old man moved some vines aside and there was something shiny. A mirror? A thinkhive plate?

"Hold my hand," the old man said.

Somehow, Jatis trusted him. It must have been the antique lilt that so echoed the women of Dromek Vornã.

"This is a displacement plate," the old man said. "It's hidden, yet not hidden. Now you know where it is, and you will always be able to come here again. Now, hold tight. Squeeze yourself against me—the field is narrow."

"Where are we going again?" Jatis said. "This makes me … queasy."

"I already told you. Another world."

And he was already sinking into the mirror-stuff of the displacement plate. Before he knew it Jatis saw his own hand disappear and the arm up to his elbow. The old man was gone but Jatis felt a sharp yank and he was through.

'This isn't another world," he said. "It's got the same sky, the same moons."

And yet it was.

For one thing, it was quiet. They were in an empty street. The wall stretched in both directions; there was a curve to it; they were in some kind of … secret zone … in the distance, the Lake of Loons, but somehow different; the water reflected only the moons and the loons, and not the kaleidoscopic lights of Aírang. The place they stood in was a small plaza; ahead, there was half a building, crystalline, like a flower with a broken stem.

A few people. But they didn't look the same. Their garments were definitely unfashionable; even the poorest slum child in Aírang had a sense of trying look smart—if only to be able to better fleece the *dorezdas*.

It was the smell that convinced him that this *was*, in its way, another world.

The air was redolent of ... something his mother had cooked once, when she was in one of her rare good moods.

An circle in a mural irised open and they stepped into some kind of tavern, but it wasn't the kind Jatis had practically been raised in. It was not noisy, nor did intoxicating fumes seep out of dark corners. There were floor cushions, in pairs, spatially separated, so this was not so much a place for congregating as for deep and private conversations. There were few patrons, and when they spoke to each other it was indistinguishable murmuring.

A servocorpse came and set two bowls down on the low table between them. It bowed. The fragrance was overwhelming: a dark, dusky, musky perfume that emanated from a warm, mud-colored broth. There seemed to be a ritual; the old man picked up the bowl in both hands, lifted up and murmured a few words before drinking deeply.

"What did you say?"

"Airos kokh'tásieh; ektáshila shiklát," the old man said. "Love is the highest joy, the lesser is chocolate."

Jatis repeated the words, and drank.

It touched his tongue and he experienced a flood of inner warmth, of something akin to love; tastes mingled, bitter, smooth, sweet, velvet.

He looked at the old man with different eyes. The old man smiled a little, wiping the drops from his beard with a fold of his cloak. "This is made from a species of bean that, according to legend, grew on the very first human world," he said, "the Homeworld of the Heart. It contains, they say, substances that send messages to the brain of wellness, of being loved. Here, on Urna, it was cultivated since the Inquestral conquest."

"What's Urna?

"Urna is a planet. An Inquestral backworld, it seems, because in became a pawn in two different games of *makrúgh* by accident. And because the High Inquest can never contradict itself, and because two planets cannot occupy the same space ... how old is Alykh?"

"How would I know?" Jatis said. "I've never been to school. A trillion sleeps?"

"Alykh is exactly as old as you are, Jatis," the old man said. A century before that, another Alykh *fell beyond* in a game of *makrúgh,* and its people, those who survived, were placed in stasis into people bins ... along with a seed that could grow a new Alykh much like the old ... waiting for a favorable world to be emptied. But the world it was destined for was not empty, after all. It only one city and a handful of villages; somehow it had got lost in the memory of the galactic thinkhives.

"To most of the people in Aírang, there was a momentary disruption of their lives, and suddenly the stars and moons and the color of the sky was a little different, but the world they awoke from stasis to was essentially still theirs. Not so for me. Or your mother."

"Who are you? What are you to her?"

"What am I to her? Only one who worships from afar. My name is Arbát, and I am a musician. This place is a place where one hears music."

As if on cue, soundcubes in the corners of the chamber lit up. A tremulous high pitched music sounded, at first more like the stridulations of night-insects. Beneath it, almost at the threshold of pitch, was a sound so deep and so slow-moving it was like how you might imagine a mountain might sing ... or a whole planet. But between the two extremes ... there came a melody.

The instrument was plucked, yet it seemed like singing. A plucked string cannot grow in intensity but must die away; it takes air from within the artist to make sound grow, but these plucked sounds did grow, and they echoed, and they sighed; they were plaintive as reeds, hollow as flutes. How could such sounds be possible?

"Who is the musician?" Jatis said. "How could he play like that? Where did all this feeling come from?"

And Arbát laughed, and said, "It's me."

Slowly, Jatis started to say something. He almost stopped himself, but this had to be true. *This man abandoned me with my mother. And she hates me and never gives a reason. It has to be true. And the way he looks at me.* Finally he made himself say it. "My mother isn't really my mother, is she? And ... you're my father."

"Forgive me," Arbát said. And then he laughed. A big laugh but a kindly one. "I could never presume to be your father," he said. "Why would you think so?"

"You have to be my father. The way you look at me. You gave me money. And sweets. But you haven't tried to fuck me."

"Jatis, you have all the wisdom of a child of the streets, yet you are innocent of so much. You've both hurt me and flattered me at the same time." And as quickly as he had laughed, the old man began to weep. "As for the one, I would not dare. I've made that kind of mistake before. As for the other, I would not presume."

"Don't cry, Arbát," Jatis said. And he hugged the old man, tentatively, and kissed him on the cheek. Which, for some reason, made him weep even more. If he wasn't like one of those *dorezdas* who sought pleasure and thought nothing of exploiting the poor, if he wasn't secretly the boy's father, who was he?

"You don't understand, do you, Jattikeh," Arbát said — only his mother ever called him by his child-name! — "How could you know? The love I feel for you, it's not a father's love … nor is it some twisted longing, for I am so old now that any twists in my desires have long unravelled." And Jatis could only look at him, more and more confused, realizing that the old man himself did not know exactly how he felt. Arbát was about to say more, but then all he said was, "So much, so much I need to impart to you."

"But if you are not my father, *what* will you be to me?"

"I sincerely hope and pray that you will allow me to be your teacher."

"And what will you teach? How to make chocolate?" That *would* be a useful skill, Jatis thought, since it seemed to be a drug that made men quite pliable.

"Ah no, Jattikeh, no. I will teach you an ever better way to move men's souls. I will give you the gift of music."

***

Downstairs, in the atrium of their dwelling, the ladies of Dromek Vornã were preparing to go out. They were chattering, comparing clients, being made up by meticulous servocorpses or painting each other's palms with a confection of ground *garámander*.

Jatis had not been sulking. But he had returned from the world called Urna more thoughtful; he had been keeping to himself. He knew that just sitting in a corner was enough to irk Éluma, but he could not help himself.

"She really is your mother … in her own fashion," is how Arbát had explained it, thereby explaining nothing at all.

The sensations that day — the mysterious voice that seemed to call to him from another space, beside the Lake — the aroma and texture of chocolate, intoxicating yet not dulling the senses — the crazy yet somehow convincing stories Arbát told — and most of all, the music he had heard. Which, it seemed, he could remember, note for note.

"If you're just going to sit and sulk, Jattikeh, go and play with your friends."

"I just want to sit. I'm not sulking."

A woman, outlandishly huge, and wearing enough layers of clingfire, irydicene and kaleodoweave to supply a fabric stall in the *suq*, popped up on the displacement plate in the floor.

"That plate is locked," Éluma said.

"I have a key."

"Still, it's appalling to displace *into* someone's home, even if you have a key. In my culture, *harám*, too."

"You superstitious bitch," the woman said.

To the women in the room, Éluma said, "Leave us for a few minutes." They left, tittering, but Jatis did not leave. He huddled in a shadowed corner. She did not notice him, even though she had barked at him earlier. This must really be an ill-omened person, he thought.

"Welcome to my establishment," his mother said. "You must be very important for Lang viHurak to have given you a secret key to this ... dwelling."

"Whorehouse," the woman said. "Or ... what is it you primitives call them ... Temple of the Love Goddess."

"The primitivity is, supposedly, the main attraction."

The woman scoffed. "My name is Arufa v'Odmáq," she said, "and I own you."

"What are you talking about?"

"It seems that you have no head for business, Your Divinity," v'Odmáq said, "and the Tourism Department has given your contract to me. I own a chain of pleasure establishments on ten worlds. I'm here to ... make a few changes. And to collect ... certain ... what would you superstitious people call them? ... *tithes.*"

"You're a rent collector?" His mother was having difficulty grasping it, though for Jatis it seemed like the regular law of the streets. "You would exploit us? Yes, you would. It was difficult for me to adjust to your way of life — the constant counting of gipfers, and credit and usury and things we never had in—"

"Let's not speak of any planets that don't even officially exist anymore," said Arufa v'Odmáq. "The point is that your quaint little establishment has been deeded to me, and I need to turn it around ... or liquidate it."

"Liquidate?"

"Terminate, 'compassionately devive', kill, whatever you want to call it."

"You would have all our acolytes executed for failing to bring in enough income?"

The woman laughed, her jowls quivering and the rainbow lights revolving in her metalgrass hair. "We don't actually kill *people,*" she said, "just corporations." Éluma sat numb. "Your current status show a negative of one iríd, four osmia, and we can write off the hemiores, arjents, and gipfers. Given the current inflation rate, it's a pittance. But it's all right. You will all work it off, you see. And the debit will come down. As long as it comes down faster than the interest accumulates, you will be fine. Where is your cash cache?"

His mother waved a hand and subvocalized to the house's thinkhive. Figures appeared above her opened palmed, blurry in the air.

"Meagre," said Arufa v'Odmáq, "but it's a good first installment. In ten tennights I will be back for the next installment."

She too, opened her palm, and from it a virtual miniature dragon leapt, landed above Éluma's hand and instantly devoured the blurry monetary figures. It then leapt back, and leaned against its owner's chest, rubbing its stomach. "That's enough." The dragon winked out and so did its owner.

No sooner had she vanished than Jatis said, "She's lying, mother."

"Why were you eavesdropping? I told you to go out and play."

"Your debit will never catch up with your credit. You will be on the streets."

"Like you?"

"I understand them, mother. You never will ... because you're not from here!"

"What!"

Jatis recoiled, waiting for a slap that didn't come.

"What do you know? Who has been talking to you?"

"Why would you care? You hate me. You're a tired whore running a failing brothel and I'm a bastard you don't love."

"No, no — you don't understand. It's not that I don't love you, it's that you're not—"

"Not who?"

They looked at each other, two caged spirits unable to communicate. In that moment Jatis felt it again ...

... from the space between spaces....

... the stars that were not the stars....

... a snatch of an unknown song....

It seemed that Éluma came to a decision. She sighed ... almost as though relieved. "You are right," she said. "Your mother is a broke and broken woman. But not everywhere. It's time for me to take you to meet someone."

She took his hand. Her touch took him by surprise. "Come," she said to him, not without tenderness. "We are going for a walk."

Jatis's heart leapt. "I already know the way," he said softly.

Origin Stories

I have been asked more than once, "Where did the title come from?"   They meant *Light on the Sound,* because it perhaps doesn't sound like science fiction. It could be a book about synaesthesia, or perhaps a romance with a romantic love scene overlooking Puget Sound.

It's an important question in a way because the Sunless Sound isn't strictly speaking a "sound" at all. According to Wikipedia, a sound is supposed to be "deeper than a bight and wider than a fjord" but the main thing is that its connected to an ocean.

The Sunless Sound couldn't possibly be connected to any ocean, not even the Sea of Tulangdaror, because the Skywall is a weird geographical anomaly—a vast *thing* jutting out from the surface of Gallendys, penetrating high into the stratosphere and so tightly sealed that it is capable of containing within it an atmosphere from a different era in the planet's past.

The truth is that the title predated the novel and even the Inquestor series, and in a way, the geography (or Gallendography, if you will) of the planet was engineered to fit the title.

The "sound" that inspired this title is actually the Connecticut Sound.   A moment of bathos for all of you who were waiting for some exotic revelation, but I guess it is a story that I never told before.

In the days when I was ghostwriting symphonies for a humming millionaire (and I wrote *all* of that down in my memoir *Sounding Brass,* so I won't retell the tale here) I spent the long vacations from Cambridge in the United States.

Much of the time, I stayed at the home of an artist friend, her husband, a Yale historian, and their son, a young musician who played the flute and the guitar. They were an intelligent and complicated family whom I'd met when I was a teacher in a music camp in Holland and the kid was a student there. It was a strangely idyllic environment where I often felt more at peace than anywhere else (having a turbulent first two decades of existence.)

During the day, they were always at work and the kids were in school, and I watched old sitcoms while orchestrating fake nineteenth century symphonies and military marches in the style of Sousa, and once a week I would fly down to Washington to deliver my handiwork to the Pentagon. (Really, really, I've told all this elsewhere ... buy the other book.)

Each afternoon their son would get back earlier than his parents would, so he would entertain me ... sometimes by playing the guitar. One day I was helping him work out a riff that turned out to be in 5/4 time, and he started to improvise some lyrics that kept containing the words "light on the sound". And because the attic I slept in had a view of the Connecticut Sound, somehow this phrase, the view out of the attic window, and the plaintive (and slightly out of tune) quality of the young man's voice … I don't know, it all melded into a sort of icon.

When I started working on the first Inquestor novel, I had only published a few stories and each story was a discovery.   But this phrase, and this moment, had haunted me for a while—I'd say five or six years—and I basically conjured up a planet to fit the phrase.

I knew what the book was *called* long before I knew what it was *about*.

Is it a good title? I am not sure, really. It seems a bit self-conscious. I flirted with changing the title, or rather turning it into a subtitle: in order to confine the four Inquestor books into the semblance of a trilogy, I shoehorned the first two books into Parts I and II of *The Dawning Shadow*.   Somehow it didn't stick. Bantam actually put an extraneous article on the over … they made it THE *Light on the Sound* … and told me it was too late to change it. (There is no article inside the book, just on the cover.)

I don't know where that family is now. Perhaps they will resurface as I flit from place to place. I do know that the title of the book is a recurring reminder, like a fading photo in an old album, of one of the few moments that I felt at peace.

A Conlang in the Pre-Conlang Era

When I started the Inquestor series in 1978 or so (the first story came out in 1979 from *Analog* magazine) I had never heard the term *conlang* and didn't really know it existed. Not surprising since the term is first cited in 1991.

The fragments of a language that appeared in the first story, *The Thirteenth Utopia,* were brief. I just wanted something cool-sounding, and had no real thought of an underlying linguistic structure.

It occurred to me much later that I had unconsciously given the language a clear Indo-European structure:

qithe qithembara
udres a kilima shtoisti

Certainly the second line is *obviously* an Indo-European language of the "very inflected" variety. "shtoisti" on the analogy of Latin is absolutely obviously a word with a second person plural, perfect tense ending.

"Udres" is an obvious genitive case, especially since "Udara" appears throughout the text. "A kilima" is clearly a preposition following by a noun in some kind of oblique case, perhaps the ablative as in Latin.

"Qithe qithembara" which I translated as "soul, renounce suffering" we less obvious: maybe a vocative case and an imperative or subjunctive form of some kind.

This language wasn't "Inquestral highspeech" but clearly seemed ancestral or connected to it in some way. But I thought nothing much if it until a couple of stories later; the "highspeech" was mentioned from time to time, but it was in *Rainbow King* which introduced the character of Sajit who eventually becomes the poet of the High Inquest's last days, that the need for actual, meaningful language creation became evident.

If Sajit is a singer, he must have songs to sing.

The first piece of "extended" writing in the highspeech was the song that Sajit performs in the story *Rainbow King* (Asimov's SF Magazine, Feb 1981). It was the cover story with a gorgeous illustration by the much loved gay artist George Barr. I possess one of George's rough sketches for this story and would love to share it here.

This song is quoted in several of the Inquestor novels (though it has never been quoted in its entirety). It established some distinctive features of the language, for instance:

There's a *temporative* case as well as a locative case common to early Indo-European languages:

asheveraín "at the time the Dispersal took place"

There's a compound perfect tense formed with some kind of contracted form of the verb *to be* and some kind of participle:

am-plãzhet "we have wept"

There's a richness of consonants and relatively few vowels (well, only about seven, long and short) and an abundance of nasalizations, making a bit like (a fan once said to me) "Sanskrit with a Portuguese accent."

The entire language did not spring fully formed into my head. Rather, as pieces of it had to be written out, little sentence fragments popped into my mind, or individual words. But it was a question from Berkeley area reader and linguist Jan Murphy that made me realize there was a lot more to the iceberg than I thought.

She was asking a question about the subjunctive — whether such and such a word was a subjunctive or not.

And I realized that the sentences and poems I was creating purely for my own clarifcation were actually analysable by Indo-European language experts. I'd created a language that could be deciphered. Buried somewhere in the subtext of these stories was a "real" language struggling to be given a voice.

As a language spoken only by an elite, performed in by poets, used as a medium only for games of ambiguity and deceit played out by millennially-aged, jaded people, it needed to be a language that's very concentrated and flexible. It also didn't have to be an "easy" language because knowledge of High Inquestral is considered a prestige accomplishment, though planetbound people would know a few expressions and could probably struggle through a basic document to some extent. It's definitely not a *lingua franca*.

It was important that the language be sonorous, with a strong sense of melody, easily manipulated consonants, and open vowels for singing with few diphthongs

Now that the basic context of *Bhasháhokh* was in place, the snatches of song became more substantial and it became possible to actually write poetry in Inquestral. And the dreaded *rules of grammar* started rearing their ugly heads (hydra heads, for whenever one was vanquished, two more would sprout.)

The language has some things in common with Panini's treatise on Sanskrit — first, it was composed at a time when Sanskrit literature was in full bloom, yet the language itself hadn't been spoken by that many people in centuries; and second, anything not actually forbidden would be allowed.

During the period in which Sajit is composing his songs, the High Inquestral tongue too is no longer an actively growing language. It once had a complex system of declensions with various endings for each declension. But, since the underpinning logic of the declensions, the active process of sandhi by which endings get absorbed and changed by time, was no longer operative, it became the custom that the noun declension groups were ignored — any ending of the correct case from any declension could be attached to any noun stem, allowing poets a lot of leeway in scansion.

Thus, *chirarans hyemadh* means "the homeworld of the heart" but "of the heart" could as easily be any of

chitarans, chitaras, chitrans, chitari, chitrens, chitars, chitras

and even others; all these forms could be legitimately used, though the phrase *chitarans hyemadh* is a catch-phrase and in that context only that form of *chitar* would be preferred.

To understand the bewildering and exuberantly freewheeling use of just about "any ending that will scan" in Inquestral poetry, I must take you back to my childhood, and to the horrifying "Dippy" Simpson, my housemaster and Latin teacher.

Dippy was the author of Cassell's Latin Dictionary and a noted classicist. Eton, my school, is know for hiring some of the greatest scholars in their fields away from higher academe or real-life jobs in order to educate its boys. Dippy was a legendary figure, as bizarre as, yet all too much more accessible than, the Dickensian Mr. Squeers. My friend Tony Little, who was at school with me and later, ironically, became headmaster of Eton, said to me recently, "Today such a man wouldn't be allowed *near* children."

No, no, this isn't an anecdote about illicit sex acts. Dippy's crime was, if anything, far worse: he belittled young people to the point of crushing their egos into nothing.

There I was, in the 1960s, in an incredible prestigious and progressive school (yes, they wore tails, but the education itself was extremely ahead of its time) — by day, reading Wagner scores in the library, going to classes with the (even more legendary) Michael Meredith who would discuss sexual imagery in Bergman films or at the drop of a hat take the whole class to London to see Ian McKellen in *Edward II*, hanging out with, and often being taught by, brilliant people who forced one to think all the time — and by night, returning to a dank, Victorian prison presided over by a gloomy, petty tyrant to whom forgetting that "motion towards" takes the accusative case was a far worse crime than poisoning one's mother.

Never one to waste anything, Dippy had cut up the galley proofs of his Latin dictionary (those were the days they came in long sort of roll-like sheets) and used to hand out the blank side for people people to answer tests on. One always prayed that the right answer would magically be listed on the other side of the paper, but it was always some other part of the dictionary.

From the day I stepped off the BOAC plane, a little boy from a Third World country traveling alone for the first time and arriving in a freezing, snowing February, I knew that getting the right ending to a Latin verb was the most important thing in the universe.

For this man greeted me as I came through immigration with the words "What is the Latin for 'I shall have used?'

I didn't know.

My fate was sealed.

I don't know if my feelings about my old school would be so conflicted if I had found myself living in a more liberal house. I *know* that other boys were not belittled on a daily basis by a madman with absolute power over them. I envied the fact that other houses produced plays and concerts — but we did not. I despaired people in my house were denied many of the enabling features the school provided.

A few years ago, visiting and speaking to people running the place now, I realize how much I missed. But also ... how much I *didn't* miss. The *school* (as opposed to the houses) *did* produce plays and concerts and I was deeply involved in some of those as I couldn't really be prevented from doing so. Indeed, I was a member of the exclusive invitation-only Praed Society (the Eton society of poets) and secretary of the Parry Society (the exclusive music group.) The school library — that's where I discovered the complete works of Hugo von Hoffmannsthal, for instance, one of whose plays became the basis for my abortive second opera.

Had I but known the Latin for "I shall have used" that day, I would not have spent the next five years living the life of a *schlimazel!*

I would like to say that today, as I was writing this article, the Latin for "I shall have used," *usus ero*, came unbidden into my mind. It is a deponent verb — it takes passive endings while being present in meaning. The stem ends in a consonant, forcing all kinds of *sandhi* when it is conjugated (and always remembering that you have to conjugate it in the opposite *voice* of its meaning.) I don't know how much of the limited hard drive space in my deteriorating brain is filled with all these verb forms, but you can see how it was all burned in.

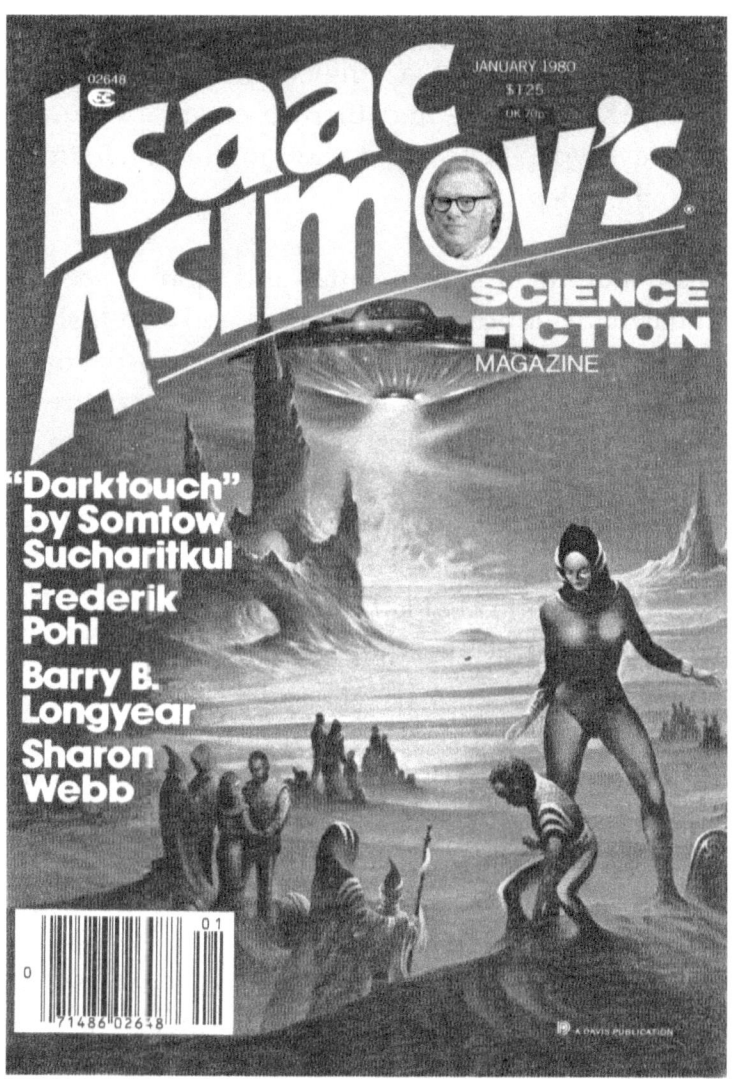

One of the joys of creating the grammar of *Bhashahokh* was to envisage a more complicated system of rules than Latin, Greek, and Sanskrit, with a verb that allowed huge degrees of variation in shade of meaning with just a single vowel shift or even moving the stress — and then to create a culture in which everyone who used the language felt free to ignore the rules at will.

To make the language softer and more susceptible to melismatic adornment, I decided early on it should have a tonic stress like earlier Indo-European languages rather than a stress accent. The stress is always marked on every word *unless* it's on the penultimate syllable (as in Spanish). This saves accents. To avoid two many diacritics, the tilde used to indicate nasalisation is assumed to carry the accent unless a different syllable happens to carry the accent. This is only true in the romanized transcription because in Inquestral script a nasalization is written as a subscript.

Vocabulary? Clearly Indo-European, but not derived from one stream of Indo-European in particular, giving the impression that the vocabulary came from many sources and was adopted during more than one period.

I could go on and on, but there won't be anything to say in succeeding appendices if I spill all the beans now.

original cover by Steve Fabian

The Web Dancer was the second of the stories I published set in the *Inquestor* world. It doesn't have characters in common with *The Thirteenth Utopia* and has a different feel to it, and it's the first one to deal with childhood which becomes one of the series' prevalent themes — even though some characters are hundreds if not thousands of years old.

Lost Tales
Darktouch

The terms were not the best.

But these were harsh times, weren't they? A war with aliens that couldn't be seen or heard. Power struggles and civil wars within the heart of the Dispersal of Man itself.

But it wasn't the prospect of the fee. Or the fatal attraction of the overcosm, that space *beyond* and *between*, where light goes wild and tantalizes you and drives you crazy with strange yearnings. Or that promise that it would only be a one-way trip in realtime, with guaranteed return by tachyon bubble, so that he would lose at most two centuries of objective time.

Kail Kirian found these conditions satisfactory. But

—for an astrogator of his ability—they were not overly tempting.

No.

It was the woman Darktouch.

The face, soft and proud, the hair jet-black, the eyes dark, the skin snow-pale as though it had never seen sun's light, the single piece of clingfire that hugged her and burned against the frail whiteness —

She was all white and black, a holosculpture of monochrome projected into a colorclashing chamber, a thing from another world.

"You'll take the offer?"

"Offer…"

Where am I? This was Lalaparalla, he remembered, the planet of warriors' rest, and he was rising from f'ang-drenched torpor, and tongues of solvent were licking in the crusts from his eyes…the war ached in his bones still, and the fang mist rOSt' once more to succor the deep hurt, to steep him in oblivion…

Ah yes. At the hostel. A message. "Request: for an astrogator of clan Kail. to take party of approximately fifty to destination Earth, terms negotiable. Whereto, Inquestral Seal."

Why request? If an Inquestral mission were involved, whv not just requisition? "You'll take the offer?" A hard voice.

And then he saw her eyes through the parting mist.

"Let me know more," he said, baffled. Such eyes!

There can't *be* a woman like this. I'm *still* in a drugged dream.

And then he saw who stood behind the woman.

Tall. A shimmercloak that glowed, pink and blue, through the dense mist. Sternfaced. *Old.*

Powers of powers! he thought. An Inquestor!

"Yours to command," he said automatically. Kirian could hardly believe he was standing so close to one, sitting naked in a f'ang bath. And one of the rulers of the Dispersal of Man! Practically a God.

"You're mistaken," said the Inquestor, and he laughed. He didn't speak with the deep-voiced authority that Inquestors had. Somehow…his voice was tender. "I cannot command you. I am no longer Ton Davaryush, Kingling of Gallendys, but merely Davaryush without-a-Clan. I am apostate. And all these people here with me…are dreamers. Refugees. They want to secede from the Dispersal of Man."

The fang…it must still be clouding his senses! "You aren't real," Kirian muttered. And he mindflicked for more solvent, to wash his eyes and clear his vision. Inquestors don't *lead* groups of crazies on *wild-goose chases.* Inquestors—

And then he saw the woman again.

There isn't such a woman.

But the dream stood there, defying him to blink her away.

"The money's good," Davaryush said. "Three thousand in tarn-crystal carat-equivalents."

"That'll sway you, if nothing else!" the woman hissed. "Mercenary!"

What's behind this woman? I feel as if I ought to take her away from this obviously lunatic Inquestor, take her to a deserted planet and—

"I don't suppose you've ever heard of Earth," said the Inquestor. "It's an abandoned place, far beyond the worlds of the Dispersal. Our ancestors came from there once. We dream about it all the time, of building a utopia there, a perfect world."

"We don't want our children to be packed off to war at six," said the woman. "We think civilization is done for."

"The alien war out there..." Davaryush said. "Do you know how many planets they've burned? Of course not. The Inquest never reveals anything..."

Kirian did not listen. He couldn't take his eyes off the woman, and her look of contempt never abated. Not once.

"Take this woman Darktouch," Davaryush said. "She is from Gallendys. Do you know of Gallendys?" Mist enveloped his mind. "No."

"You astrogators of the clan of Kail, you who mindlink with the delphinoid shipminds to guide the starships through the overcosm ... you of all people should know. Do you really know of the delphinoid shipminds, the gigantic brains that are sealed into the starships?"

"What is this?" said Kirian, uneasy. "I'm not a

historian, not a philosopher. Just tell me the terms and let me decide. I'm a soldier, an overcosm flier, a man of action."

The woman laughed once, a warm laugh. Perhaps she was not solid rock to the core, then, like a dead planet.

"Listen, then,' said Davaryush. "On Gallendys there is it gigantic volcanic crater, a hundred kilometers high, a thousand across. Within is a dense atmosphere, a relic from a previous epoch…in this dark land, above the Sunless Sound, the delphinoids float. They are creatures who are all brain. They perceive the overcosm directly, without instruments. It is this power that we use to travel between the stars.

"But listen more! These delphinoids sing, Kail Kirian. Their songs are holosculptures ten kilometers across, suspended over the perpetual darkness of the Sunless Sound. They are imagesongs, light poems woven out of overcosm visions. And a strange music too, a harmony that makes men weep, even hardened soldiers like you. Even Inquestors. For every starship that sails the overcosm, a song must die."

The mist was dying now. Davaryush's intensity touched Kirian, made him nervous. And he glimpsed other people behind, other crazies. Davaryush continued: "No human who had once seen the light on the sound, and heard the songs of the ones whose minds were turned to the space beyond our space, to the utter beauty of the overcosm…no human who had once experienced this could willingly kill a delphinoid. The Inquest understood the need for space travel. They mutated a race that was deaf and blind, and gave them a mythos and a mission, and now they live in the darkness and silence of the crater-wall caverns. And they fly out on their airships and fling their forcenets over the delphinoids and bring them home. They do not know that it is to feed the shipyards, to glorify the Dispersal of Man.

"I was Kingling of Gallendys once. This woman was a girl, a genetic throwback; she could see and hear. At puberty she joined the holy hunt, and what she saw there made her flee, half-crazed, out of the dark country to the City of Effelkang where I held power. And later she took me to see for myself. An old man and a girl. we saw the slaughter of joy. It changed us...

"We have all had these experiences. All of us."

And Kirian saw the others now, behind them: an old man; a couple of child-soldiers with laser-irises, who could have killed him with a glance and a subvocalized command; a matron; a young hermaphrodite in a whore's robe; a princeling clad in lapis and iridium; a slaveboy with a chrysanthemum branded on his forehead; a girlsinger with a whisperlyre...

They're *shameless!* he thought. *Look how they carry on, without regard for rank Look how brazenly they flout the principle of degree. The slave boy and the princeling*

held hands and were close. The hermaphrodite leaned on a
child-soldier's arm, defying all decency.

"You're shocking."

"Don't criticize," said Darktouch coldly. "Just take
the money and help us."

The Inquestor motioned her to be quiet. With such
a strange gentleness… "We are giving up anger.
Remember that." With the same voice he said to
Kirian: "We have all been through such experiences as
Darktouch has. We have all turned our backs on the
Dispersal. I say this so that you may see why I, an
Inquestor, a former Kingling, a hunter of utopias
once…have come begging to you."

Kirian was profoundly shocked. Only once before
in his life—

And then he mouthed his deepest fear. "This
Earth. Is the route well mapped? Are there any
anomalies in spacetime, any tachyon whirlpools…?"

"None are known to exist," said Davaryush. "And
moreover, I have been able to requisition power
enough for one tachyon bubble. When you have
delivered us to Earth, you may use it to return to your
homeworld."

Powers of powers! "You must have been a very
important man," said Kirian, wondering at how low
the Inquestor had fallen…

For the tachyon bubble's secret was known only to
the Inquest. They were bubbles of realspace, held
together by phenomenal power expenditure—the

deaths of suns, it was sometimes said—that smashed their way through planes even higher than the overcosm, traveling instantaneously...If Davaryush could really supply such a thing, Kirian's travel time would be halved, the problems of time dilation would not be nearly so bad.

Not that he cared about time dilation. Only a loner could be an astrogator: how could a sociable person stand it. coming home after ever trip to find his friends grown old, dead? "If it weren't for traveling with you lunatics," he said, "Ii wouldn't even hesitate."

The slaveboy and the princeling had moved closer to each other for reassurance, had their arms around each others' shoulders...intolerable!

Darktouch cried, "I told you, Daavye!" And Kirian cringed, , that a clan less woman should dare to call an Inquestor by a diminutive. "He's a mercenary, and for what we want we'll never be able to pay him. We're trampling on all he believes in. He's a cog in a machine, a rat in a maze, and he'll never know it..."

"Hold it!" Kirian said.

She turned back to look at him. The mist had parted, and she was so *real* that no overdose of fang could have created her. He wanted to touch her so badly it hurt him...but he could not even reach out. The rift between them was complete. It was not her remoteness (he sensed it was insecurity as much as anything); not her beauty. But the fact that she would not acknowledge him as a person, only as a type. Was there a brittleness behind her scorn?

Davaryush was saying, "It has to be Earth. Because it is so far away from people's minds, so that they will not search us out and kill us. And because it is the source, the place of beginning. a potent symbol out of the farthest past there can have been…"

"Don't go on talking," said Darktouch. "It's just wind to him, just noise." She was bitter; how many astrogators had they tried?

"I haven't said no yet, have I?" he said, feigning toughness.

They all edged forward like one man—

He heard their unison intake of breath; he saw the woman and the Inquestor exchange a quick look that shut him out of their topsy-turvy world and their crazy philosophy—

And felt naked, suddenly.

* * *

It was a routine journey at first.

The passengers had all opted for stasis; they would only awake on Earth. Except for Davaryush— and he was an Inquestor, who must always lead, even if dethroned—and Darktouch. That he couldn't understand. Six months subjective, in the overcosm— but he brushed her from his mind.

Or tried to. He reclined in the small room. Circular mirror walls gleamed around him. He was shielded.

He was at the ship's heart. He closed his eyes and reached out with brain-implanted sensors. It was second nature; he had been doing it since puberty.

The delphinoid shipmind came alive, moving like an ocean in darkness. The sensation was soft, familiar. Endless darkness cushions swam by. He knew the ship was easing from its orbital anchor. But he saw nothing. He was alone in the room. It was so still... *(What's it like, to be born in the dark country of Gallendys, to see the imagesongs of the delphinoids, and not to have words to protest, to understand? And how can something be so beautiful that you can't bring yourself to kill it? Killing was second nature to him, like touching the delphinoid shipmind. If commanded, could I have killed the woman Darktouch?* Kirian was no thinker. Thinking was for Inquestors. You couldn't afford to think...The delphinoid's warmth enveloped him. Then a voice, tugging at the bottom of his mind ... *Do you hear?* (An untried delphinoid. He would have to coax it, firmly, onto the right flight plan.) *I hear you,* he mindwhispered. *Are you ready? I'm afraid. This route is poorly charted...*

Be still. be still, he mindspoke, as though to a pet animal. But he was frightened too. There was always the split second of blinding terror that would come upon him, seconds before bursting into the *other* space where space and time go mad. A memory would come to him, a nightmare—

On his first war mission. He was seven years old. A newboy. Anyone could have ordered his death. A hundred starships packed into a shieldsphere, charging through the overcosm; and he was alone on a deck with the walls deopaqued and the overcosm light raging, and alarms blaring and sirens screeching and he was so alone, and—

One by one. The ships falling into darkness. So strangely beautiful....They flew into gold-tinged scarlet nets of flame, vanished, a ship at a time, like beads of a cut necklace, slipping one by one into water. And after, in another chamber, stripped and lined up and black mourning cloaks thrust over their shoulders, all the children standing stiff and frightened while the Inquestors paced and raged. Huge reflections of their shimmercloaks flapping, blushing the mirrorsilver walls...

What's happened to the other ships?

Not looking at the other children. Obeying or dying.

"It was a tachyon whirlpool."

The Inquestor's voice rasping above his head. And Kirian could almost touch the silence. More pacing, and the floor humming eerily as the Inquestor's fursoles rubbed and whispered. A child burst out crying. He clenched his eyes. The boy would be returned to homeworld in disgrace. *Impassive. Make your face impassive.*

Another Inquestor's voice: "Never forget this experience until the day you die! Tachyon whirlpools were made by man.

"During the first experiments in tachyon travel there were foolish errors. A thing that travels faster than light, like a tachyon, must have a negative timeflow relative to our universe! And the first experimenters were hurled into the past, twisting the local continuum, wrenching causality apart. And even now these tachyon whirlpools remain, symbols of their lust for knowledge! Repeat this! It is good that only the Inquest knows the secret of tachyon travel."

Unison chorus: *It is good that only the Inquest knows the secret of tachyon travel.*

"It is evil to question nature. Only the Inquest is wise."

It is evil—

Theirs was the only ship to survive.

And later they burst into realspace in the region of the star Keima, and they obliterated the planet Zelterkangh. It had been a simple punitive expedition, nothing a single starship couldn't handle...

The terror lived again for a moment in the ship's darkness. Even after twenty years. More vividly this time than the other times...

So it isn't a perfect universe. That much my lunatics have gotten right. But they're wrong to run away from it. They shouldn't question the way things are. Man is a fallen being after all, he thought.

Quickly he returned the memory to its cage.

You can't hurt me, he lied to himself.

The nightmare beat at the cage bars. This time it came mingled with the eyes of the woman Darktouch. He beat it back. And the darkness of the shipmind did take him, eventually, but not before he had gazed into the strange woman's eyes for a long time, puzzling himself…

* * *

Some weeks later, he broke free from the shipmind and staggered up to the observatory.

She was alone there. All the walls were deopaqued. They stood on the metallic floordisk, floating in—

The overcosm raged. Oppressing him. No escape from it.

And she was a silhouette gazing out, not moving. Even her clingfire garment was muted by comparison with it. She didn't acknowledge him, only stared out at the

—*vermilion hurricanes spattering whitepeaked wavecrests, the ochre lightpeaks tumbling, crumbling over blindingwhite catherinewheel firevolleys*—

"You mustn't expose yourself to the overcosm too long." She flinched from the words, startled. "You'll stare your eyes into cinders." He went on, not liking the silence, "People have gone mad, you know, from being unable to cope with the torrent of sensations—"

"It's beautiful." She turned her back on him.

—*geysers of green flame gushing through scarlet walls, veils that ripped to reveal more veils*—

"It's just nothing, just mass hallucinations, because we can't understand what we perceive." Damn it, why did she ignore him? "You spend all our interstellar trips like this?"

"Always. I am afraid of stasis." She was frail in the colorstorm.

"They're just lights."

"The world the delphinoids see, Kirian. Isn't it strange?" She turned and watched him; he wanted her then, and despised her too, and could think of nothing to say. Finally he said, "You're so full of words. As though words could save the universe. Like this utopia of yours ... more words."

"You poor mercenary..."

"Don't pity me! You reject reality, you dream hopeless dreams—"

"Of love, brotherhood, things like that..." She began to explain it all to him, and it was like a child's wishful thin kings, impractical, destructive. "Oh. I see you're not impressed. How could you be? They've lied to you so much you couldn't recognize a truth to save your own skin."

"To be so sure of something..." he said. He saw how her eyes shone, how she seemed to be looking straight through him, to some world she and the others had made up. "You're not perfect either," he said brusquely.

"Of course not! But—"

"Oh, you're so proud. You see not what I am, but what I'm supposed to be like in your eyes, and—"

She turned away sullenly. No, she was no angel.

—*volcanohearts twisted inside out, lightfeathers fluffed out of prismpools fracturing into mosaics*—

"Why shouldn't I hate your kind?" she burst out. "Don't you know how you make the delphinoids suffer, how every moment of their lives from the moment they are mindsoldered into the ships is spent in excruciating agony, how you force them to live when they can't sing, which is agony beyond your understanding?"

"Intellectually one knows—"

"Every parsec we've advanced across the Dispersal of Man has given unconscionable agony to a sentient creature! How can you live with that? How can we all live with that? If you can live with it, you must be—"

It was true. But it had always been the way. There were no alternatives.

In the end he said, "Are the imagesongs even more beautiful than this?"

Not looking at him, she said, "Of course. They are art, and this, though beautiful too, is random lightnoise…"

She's the first woman ever to despise me! I'm not a role, I'm a human being! he thought. And she was so still.

Like a holosculpture in a museum: untouchable.

You're proud, so proud it goes against all your fine talk about love and brotherhood. You're hypocritical as the rest of us.

Above them, the firestorm stretched to forever. Behind the stormshards, past the colorclouds, pale sinuous snakes of light darted from dark to dark.

And he was jealous of the certainty for which Darktouch had given up the whole galaxy. And jealous of the lunatics who had stolen her from him...

So he fled and sought the comfort of the shipmind's darkness, and drew the darkness over his thoughts as a child retreats into a blanket heavy with familiar smells, retreats from the fear of night.

He even welcomed the recurring nightmare of the tachyon whirlpool. ..that at least was familiar.

    * * *

Many months later, from out of the darkness

—he burst blind through terror that didn't belong there at all, his mind screaming burning ANOMALY ANOMALY against the relentless logic of the shipmind, and he was crushed into darkness within darkness screaming falling burning ANOMALY ANOMALY—

(Memory: a hundred ships dropping into the net of flame.)

"Cut the connection!"

(Memory: alone on deck with the sirens bawling.)

The shipmind said, *Kail Kirian, we have navigated safely past the tachyon whirlpool.* A toneless internal whisper.

"Identify the anomaly," he said, "for the last time."

It is a tachyon whirlpool. Kirian. What else can I say?

(A f'ang dream?) "If that's true, we're off course."

No.

"Yes! This should be the vicinity of Earth, and the failed tachyon experiments were millennia after the first Dispersal from Firstworld!"

I understand this. I understand the unlikelihood. Nevertheless, what I sense I sense.

"How can there be whirlpools in this uninhabited, abandoned sector? You're malfunctioning—"

No.

Kirian broke the connection finally. And passed through the forcecurtain to the observatory. She was still there; it was almost as though minutes, not months, had elapsed.

—firebubbles foamed through lacelightcurtains lanced by liquid lightnings—

The old man was there too. His shimmercloak blushed softly against the patches of night.

Darktouch turned around.

He gaped at her. The light from the overcosm haloed over her face, the hair flowed dark and free, the cling fire kissed her slight body. He couldn't speak.

"Well?" Davaryush said. "We felt...disturbance."

"Tachyon whirlpool." Mustn't sound frightened. Mustn't give anything away!

"That's—" said Darktouch.

"I know! I know it's impossible!"

The Inquestor merely said, "Will it delay us much?"

Is that all they can think about, their fool mission? And Darktouch moved closer to him, and his desire embarrassed him. "Not long."

"Good," she said. Fanatic eyes, shining...

"I don't share your dream," he said angrily. "I just want to get to the bottom of this anomaly."

"Mercenary!"

"You should go into stasis!" he shouted. "The strain's getting to you—"

"Darktouch," the Inquestor interrupted, "scorn, hate, all the things we are giving up." .'

She subsided. Behind her, the lightveils parted—

—kaleidoscoped, dissolved—

Darkness fell without warning.

"WHAT HAVE YOU DONE?" he shouted.

Another whirlpool! said the ship. The mind connections closed all around him, the darkness breathed on him, mathematical figures danced and wavered in his head—

　　* * *

Afterwards, they burst out of the overcosm into a blackness of new stars. One in particular, a yellow dwarf of no importance. Realspace was dull compared with the overcosm, so Kirian stayed in his wombchamber, assessing the damage. It was bad. Very bad.

The utopians didn't have a chance.

The stasis-pod life-support systems had been thrown into dysfunction. They were all dead: the princeling, the slave boy, I he girl with the lyre, the hermaphrodite, all of them with their hope-fired eyes and their fa_se, poignant dreams...

The tachyon bubble system was dead too. He would have to use the delphinoid to return home. He would lose four centuries to time dilation, not two.

Before he went to the observatory he opaqued the walls. HI! felt more comfortable between the gray walls...

"You have to go back."

They looked blankly at him. They could have been holosculptures of the dead.

"Look, the last tachyon whirlpool—it wiped out all your chances. Even though I still can't believe it was there at all. The dormant passengers are permanently dead. You can't create a viable colony. You can't ever propagate the species—you must be over three hundred years old, Davaryush."

"Four hundred and twelve."

He felt a sudden compassion for their shattered dream. Bul pushed it aside. "The shipmind can think us home readily enough," he said. "It's learned where the two anomalies are..."

"No!" said Darktouch. "Not while we still have one male left—" And she glanced at Kirian, hostile.

Oh no! I desire her. but not like this....

"Now wait!" he said angrily. "I'm no head-in-the-clouds utopian like you and the Inquestor. I know where I belong. I've finished my part of the bargain. You've failed, and I'm sorry for you, and I can take you home at no extra charge. I can't leave an old man and a woman to fend for themselves on a dead planet —"

"Never! Not after the agony the delphinoid has been through to bring us here!" cried Darktouch, trembling. "We vowed to let it die, to free it from its shipbonds!"

He saw that she was assessing him now, as genetic material, as a piece of meat, a pawn in her utopia...He wanted to help her so badly, in spite of her hate. She couldn't want to stay. It was beyond all reason, even a fanatic's.

"I want to go back to what I know," he said.

"With the war and the civil war," said Davaryush, "I think it's rather an ambiguous question as to whether there will be a Dispersal to return to..."

I can't accept that! "No!"

"All right," said Darktouch calmly. "We'll land on Earth. Then you can impregnate me and leave. You do desire me, don't you? I am beautiful, aren't I?" And then she began to weep, terrible, hysterically.

But he was afraid to comfort her.

"Delphinoids don't make mistakes…" he said.

"Don't speak of delphinoids again!" she screamed.

"It will pass," said the Inquestor gently. "You will never understand what she has suffered on Gallendys…"

"Blank out the walls!" she cried out. "I want to see Earth! I want to see the dream!"

Abruptly the starstream burned in darkness behind her. She turned and stared out at the tiny yellow disk. He tried to put his arms around her, but she was like a statue.

"Remember the delphinoid's pain," she said quietly. Her eyes said, *Animal!*

Davaryush's voice came from behind them: "You see the desperation that drove us, Kail Kirian. You *must* let us down on Earth; and then, if you choose to go, we will at least die on the ground that made us, on the planet untouched by the Inquest…"

And he was moved, in spite of himself.

The inconvenience of it! He longed to be in battle where he belonged. Here they were as far from the center of things as it Was possible to be, as far as the very primordial beginnings of Man. Even the stars were thin here, in this wisp of galactic arm; it was a bleak and desolate sky. Cold touched his spine.

"Very well," he heard himself say. 'I'll land you there, then ship back to my homeworld. Even though abandoning you goes against my conscience."

"Oh," said Darktouch, mocking him, "do you have one?"

But she thanked him with her eyes., *I will not touch her,* he thought, *while she still hates me, but perhaps I can find a way. ....*

"Look, Earth," said Davaryush. They smiled, both of them, falling into their dream. *How could they smile when there was* no *hope? How could they?*

Earth hung in the blackness: opalescent, white-blue, beautiful, dead.

    * * *

Desert. Rocky desert, hilly desert, dune deserts, deserts of blasted glass that might have been cities fused together in some cataclysm ... harsh polar caps made ice deserts. Millennia before, men had done a good job of killing Earth...

In the north of one of the great landmasses they found thin grass-fields, yellow-gray and stubblestrewn, and the lander settled on a hill-fringed plain where a brook ran to merge beyond the horizon with a shallow river. The lander sprouted wheels—Kirian realized with a shock that here they could not

travel from place to place by displacement plates—
and waited.

The three of them stood by the stream. Why, they
didn't even know how to set up a camp or forage for
food, thought Kirian, any of the skills that a Kail
learned from childhood.

"I'd better help you find food," he said, avoiding
their eyes:

But they were watching their new planet,
enraptured.

Food they found readily enough. On the foothills
were fruit trees with reddish round fruit and soft
yellow meat; and curious, fearless fish fairly leapt into
their forcenets from the brook.

They'll live an idyllic life, thought Kirian, *without my
help.*

Until they die.

He didn't want to admit that he feared the four-
hundred-year time dilation and the tachyon
whirlpools that didn't belong...*I mustn't leave in
unseemly haste,* he thought.

The next day they went exploring. They climbed
the hills easily. Davaryush followed on a floater
because of his age and because the gravity was a
shade higher than he was used to.

Darktouch was silent the first few hours.

He would look at her when she didn't know he
was looking and see her somehow at peace. She no
longer groomed her hair, so it streamed free in the

wind; the clingfire garment was worn threadbare. It gave off no fire but a pearly rainbow. She belonged here.

The ground was soft, yielding to his feet. It was a strange sensation, quite unlike the continual disruptions of displacement plates.

It would take days, months, to explore the world. But from what they could see around them it was truly dead. Twenty millennia had rubbed the planet smooth. They saw no sunken cathedrals such as the sand acropolises of war-torn Kellendrang, no mile-high husks of skyscrapers such as bestrode the firesnowed horizons of Ont...

At the summit he said, awkwardly, "I wish there was not this gulf between us."

"I pity you, Kail Kirian," she said, avoiding his eyes. "You belong to the old things, cruel and senseless. You've no pride in yourself—otherwise why would you have come here for mere money? If you could only see things as they are—"

"If only you could!" he retorted. "You're just as hypocritical as the rest of the human race. You took my help, didn't you? Help in running away. You're cowards. Running away-to die!"

They glared at each other. Her hair blew across her face. *How softly she glows,* he thought, *against the strange yellow light of this sun.*

Davaryush, ahead of them, called out. Kirian eased himself over the hillcrest and rested his elbows on a flat boulder, and his field of vision telescoped abruptly to an endless brown plain spattered with smooth sand-carved rockshapes like sculpted bushes. Half-way to the horizon was a forest of brown trees... trees?

"What are they?" he said.

"Let's go and see," Darktouch answered. He felt an unbecoming curiosity in himself for a moment. "Well, don't you want to find out? Why, they look almost like...people, those trees."

"It's too far to walk," he said, and summoned two more floaters with a flick of his mind.

They rode the breeze, the two of them, down through the desert. It was so far...sand stretched until distance meant nothing any more. And the wind-etched sandstone sculptures...they were huge, bigger even than the delphinoid that orbited above them, waiting.

They were dwarfed by this one plain. And the thought that the huge world stretched around them forever. Kirian felt lonely. From ground level they could not see their objective at all, so they floated blindly, trusting the floater settings.

And then there were—

People.

***

Kirian stepped gingerly off his floater. He practically walked into a man. The man was quite cold and he didn't move.

There were other men standing nearby. Farther off, some women. Many were naked. These had on nothing but a blue strap around their wrists. Others had clothes. Clingfire was one of the fabrics, but the fire was frozen. Others were in fantastical costumes, headdresses with pointed layers, extravagant codpieces.

They didn't move.

"What is this?" Kirian felt panic. "First the tachyon whirlpools, now this—holosculpture museum, on a planet with no people. This is the wrong planet!"

"Delphinoids don't lie," Davaryush mocked him, gently.

"You don't like mysteries, do you, mercenary?" said Darktouch, and smiled a hard smile.

"No, I don't," said Kirian. "I like answers! We've got to get back now if we can. Obviously we had a warped shipmind and we're somewhere quite different from where we set out for. Maybe you plan to die here, but I'm leaving."

"Coward!" Darktouch shouted.

"I'm no coward! I've killed more men than you've ever seen! But I'm going to go back to what I do understand."

The statues never moved. He slammed his fist hard on a woman's shoulder; it was harder than a starship's hull.

"You're all alike," said Darktouch bitterly. "You want no mysteries. You've no pride in being humans. Inside, you hatp youselves!"

Her anger sounded small on the huge plain. Kirian looked around him. Perhaps a thousand humans, frozen hard and seemingly indestructible. Children, too. He touched a child near him; red-haired, the hair tousled but stiff as metal.

Red hair, like mine, he thought. The thought irritated him. obscurely ... something oddly familiar about the child...he stared at the unseeing eyes.

He did want to know what they were.

Maybe there's no harm in asking one question ....

"All right," he said. "I'll stay a few days more. We can run tests on the statues. Maybe this is a hall of fame, an ancient artifact, an Inquestral plot, a cunning mirage...When we've found the answer I'll leave."

And he surprised himself, that he was able to wonder...Were they humans somehow frozen out of time? Or imitations of humans, bait laid by some alien?

And why do they seem so familiar?

Afterwards he closed his eyes and used the delphinoid, whose orbit matched their position, monitoring them constantly, to move the landing craft to the edge of the forest of statues and set up the shelters.

But he found that the order to the delphinoid was not a simple reflex as it had always been: for the first time, a thought nagged at him: *This ship is in agony, and cannot die.*

* * *

He woke to the dawn. The sands had shifted; the statues had not moved at all, and some were now knee-deep in little dunes.

The dawn—here it was like pink feathers of a pteratyger, speared and brought down over the gray sea on Keneg, Kirian's homeworld. The image chilled him; he did not think he could still be homesick.

This planet did have a magic then…it was the primal homeworld.

He shut the shelter door and approached the nearest statue. For they must be statues, if they didn't move—statues from a time of primitive technology that had stood the ravages of twenty millennia. Impossible.

He and Darktouch worked on the statues that morning. They wanted to saw off a piece-part of a garment, they had decided, just in case the statues were real people—and they were trying an old man's white tunic. A pretty tableau watched them, a young woman and two boys all in white. Their metal tools all broke on the cloth. It never gave so much as a micron, from what their instruments could tell them.

In one of the pauses she said to him: "Did you ever figure out why the tachyon whirlpools were there'?"

"I suppose our history is wrong. The Dispersal of Man is too large for full records, perhaps. The abortive experiments were so long ago, and—"

"But the whirlpools are anomalies in space and time, aren't they? So they could be experimenters in the future?"

"Rather hypothetical. considering your sort think the future is pretty much done for."

"You've no imagination. What could I have expected." But the insult was automatic, not laced with spite as it might have been two days before. They worked on without talking.

It was hard to take his eyes off her. Long crimson-tinged shadows crossed her face...*If I don't leave, immediately, I'll...fall in love with her.* And the thought was like pain.

After the laser device had failed to chisel off a piece of the man's clothing, they rested, leaning against the hard statues. A light wind sprang up, sprinkling them with sand.

"You've never had any experience," Darktouch said, "to make you doubt the universe you were taught to believe in?"

"No,"

—but there were the hundred ships falling into the tachyon whirlpool—

"Not even war?"

"War is necessary! It keeps the children occupied, it purifies the human instincts, it keeps down the population..."

—I blasted one of the revivified corpses over and over and still he came barreling towards me. I blew off his head and he collapsed a centimeter from my face...my first kill—

"You don't believe that."

"The Inquest told me!"

—and the headless torso of the kindled corpse, still groping towards me across the starship's silver floor, struggling without a mind, and me striking it over and over in my nine-year-old passion, yelling hot anger from my heart—

Kirian was in tears, suddenly.

—and the hundred starships falling

—and after, on leave, going to Alykh, the pleasure planet, riding the varigrav coasters until we were drunk with giddiness, and then on to the oblivion of f'ang and Lalaparalla . ..and then another war and another—

He didn't want to think of himself. He didn't know who he was, anymore. "Why are you called Darktouch," he said, "in the hightongue, and not a pretty name from an archaic language?"

"Because," she said, "in the dark crater over the Sunless Sound there are no names. People speak with their hands. I did not know I could have a name, until I went on my first hunt and saw and heard…

"They're not delphinoids to us, they're—" she did a fingerdance across his palm then. "Huge, sleek, streamlined creatures that are all brain. They talk by drawing patterns of light in the dark air above the Sound. And they leap and soar and sing, they sing!

"We had netted one and were towing him home in the airship. Their bodies were twined around each other, singing of victory. And then he began to sing. The lightstrands tore the air apart. It was pure tragedy…of course you have to be deaf and blind to hunt them! At lightsend I ran away, crawling through the hidden tunnels till I reached the light world, struggling across the badlands of Zhnefftikak until I reached the city where men could see and hear, Effelkang…"

Kirian turned his back on her and began to laser the man's tunic again. "I'm not responsible for the sins of the Inquest," he said. "You're just trying to make me feel guilty so I'll stay here and join with you in a loveless breeding plan and make your project come true…"

"No!"

But he *was* feeling guilty.

"Look," he said at last, "they all have these blue bracelets in common…maybe if we lasered a bracelet." By noon there was still no result. By then Kirian felt an overpowering need to find the answer to the riddle. "How about this one?" He indicated a boy standing behind the old man. "His bracelet seems a little askew." A red-haired boy, that odd familiar look. unnerving somehow…Kirian tugged at the bracelet. The boy sprang to life. "Where is this?" he shrieked, looking wildly around him. "Where's the space station?"

Darktouch was beside him quickly, trying to calm him.

"What?" said Kirian. "He speaks the hightongue?" They took the boy to the shelter, kicking, screaming, and biting all the way.

    * * *

The shelter: a circular silver wall around them. Like a room on the starship.

The boy: eleven or twelve. The age of a young warrior of the Dispersal. That familiar look—Kirian could almost put his finger on it. But no…

"Who are you?" he demanded. The boy shrank back, still defiant. He tried to break free of the tranquilizer field—

"Let me out of here! This is the wrong planet I guess; there's no space station, and I didn't fasten my stasis bracelet tight enough—"

He stopped. He looked into Kirian's face. And then he said, "I'm dreaming." And then he smiled. The smile made Kirian uneasier than ever.

And then Davaryush smiled too. And Darktouch. They were all smiling, threatening Kirian with some secret knowledge—

"I'm getting out of here!" he said, trapped. "I'm calling the delphinoid now—"

The fear was gone from the boy. He looked at Kirian with a strange reverence…almost as if Kirian were some prince, some … Inquestor even. "I'm not afraid now," the boy said. "This is the dawn time; I understand that I've accidentally triggered the bracelet thing by tying it wrong on Sirius. What a stroke of luck I've found you! Now you can do it up properly for me and bundle me off to the station and I can get home. Right?"

Kirian released the tranquilizer field. "Tell me what's happening, someone?" he said desperately.

The boy laughed, a silvery laugh that somehow made his throat catch…"Ha! Well…I guess you really wouldn't know. Would you? Davaryush, Darktouch, and Kirian?"

"Now, answers," Kirian said tightly. The boy had known his name. What next?

"Be gentle," said Darktouch. She moved closer to Kirian, and their hands touched and were warm together. "Where are you from?"

"Sirius."

"Where—?" Kirian said.

"It's a colony. My parents sent me back to Earth to go to school."

"To this empty planet?" said Kirian, more and more bewildered.

"Well, it is the dawn time. The stasis field—"

"All right," said Davaryush. The boy turned and stared at him, huge-eyed. "You recognize us." The boy nodded slowly. "So you must be from the future, from a time when Earth is populated again, with a colony or two even."

He nodded again.

"We're a little simple," Davaryush said, "to sophisticated people from the future like you. So why don't you tell us in easy language, what's happened, what you're doing here…"

"Simple!" the boy blurted out, awestruck. "You of all people, Davaryush, you, how can you possibly say that?" And he seemed moved.

"I'm old," Davaryush said; and Kirian saw that his face was not tired the way old men's faces are; it was aglow with wonder. "If I tell you everything," said the boy, "will you take me back to the space station and do up my bracelet properly?"

"Of course."

"Well then—"

Kirian could not forget the story.

* * *

More than a thousand years ago, the fathers had come, fleeing an intolerable world: Davaryush, Kirian, Darktouch. Men filled the whole galaxy; but great wars decimated them, and broke the web of power that the Incuest had spun over the million worlds of the Dispersal of Man...

Davaryush and Darktouch and Kirian came with their dream of a new humanity. They came and rekindled the Earth.

There were great secrets of science in the old days. Men knew how to compress a fragment of spacetime into a tachyon bubble, and send it flying instantaneously through space ... It was a lost secret. The children of the utopians did not recover all the knowledge of the past. But they felt a longing for the stars, a longing common to all men. A way was found, without the tremendous energy of tachyon bubbles. Men were sent through space through the tachyon universe, with its negative time-flow, in a time-stasis shield which locked the traveler into the moment of his departure, preventing time paradoxes until reality could recapitulate to the same moment...

The plain of statues was a gigantic space station, a harbor. But its walls and its machinery were not built yet, nor was the huge town of Kirian-Angkar beside the station. One day the domes would come, and the towers of a great city.

How had they known they would succeed? How had they picked the site of the space station? It was easy. For they had grown up seeing the passengers standing in the sand, in their millennia of sleep...

And how had the earliest people known who the travellers were? There was a legend of a young boy with his stasis-bracelet askew, who had accidentally awoken in the dawn time and spoken with the ancestors…

    * * *

I'm the boy!" the boy was shouting. "And to think my parents named me after the boy in the myth—"

Davaryush said, thoughtfully: "Science is strange. We had the technology to do all this in our own civilization. But it never occurred to them to use tachyon travel for mass journeys…because above all, the Inquest wanted power, exclusive power, over the Dispersal of Man. We didn't have tachyon travel for everyone because the Inquest could not bear to give up one iota of its terrible power!"

Darktouch added: "The rules of the universe don't change But the uses to which they're put…our children *did* learn—will learn—from our dream, Davaryush! To work for the good of all … Our hopeless dreams of freedom and love—are vindicated, Kail Kirian!" '

It was too much for Kirian to take. *Got to get home…*

"You'll stay now, Kirian," said Darktouch. "I can't, I can't!" He blacked out desperately and groped for the shipmind in the sky. *Homeworld! I want homeworld!*

And the three of them were laughing, roaring with laughter—

"You're staying, Kirian. Not a doubt of it," said Davaryush.

"Of course not! You must have tricked me...

The silver walls returned to his vision.

"Tricked you, Kirian?" said Darktouch. "Just look at the boy, Kirian, just look at the boy!" And he did. The boy. Standing against the wall. A redhead with unkempt hair, a slight, insignificant sort of boy...there were a million boys like him, scrabbling in the ruins of burnt cities, hawking sweet sin the bazaars of Alykh, staring wide-eyed at the delphinoid starships that streaked across the night skies of their homeworlds... he saw nothing remarkable.

Until he saw his own face, reflected in the wall beside the boy's. Distorted by the wall-curve, and yet so alike...

"You're my...I mean, I'm your—"

"Forefather," the boy whispered, and knelt down to kiss his hand. As though he were a visiting Inquestor...

He trembled with pride. Then he raised the child up and gazed at the face until he could see, behind the features that mimicked his own, traces of Darktouch's face, too.

Darktouch, who had despised him, who had accused him of hating himself, of being without pride, of being senseless and meaningless and cruel...but he knew now how to make her love him.

And thought of the delphinoid, orbiting above them, in its terrible pain.

* * *

Darkness. A terrible loneliness.

Kirian's mind was blank, joined to the shipmind. The darkness pressed against him, waiting.

"Shipmind," he called softly, "what is it you really feel? Can you not share it with me?"

And he felt pain. Like nails being driven into his head, over nd over, into his spine, into his bones, his body rolling in a barrel of nails, pain beating burning blasting bursting him and more a ails driving driving into him everywhere and screaming until he would never stop screaming until he screamed himself into silence ... nails nails nails nails nails ...

And behind the pain, a still grief. The grief of the Sunless Sound whispering under the hunters' airships. The grief of lost songs. Of unborn torrents of light in the thick dark sky. And Kirian wept until he was beyond tears—

Nails nails nails—

And pity behind the grief. Pity for a being so pitiless it could torture a sentient creature. Compassion for him.

Kirian's mind whispered, "Shipmind, I'm sorry. I knew, but I tried not to know. Go free now."

***

He awoke to night. Darktouch was standing by the shelter under the strange thin starlight. He came to her…"I freed the shipmind," he said. "I think he's going to die now."

Darktouch said, "I tried to hate you so much! Because all soldiers were supposed to be mindless automata, slaves of the Inquest! But you do have compassion after all…"

"Glimpsing the future has changed so much." They were silent. The air was heavy with the tension of beginning relationships. He said, suddenly, "I can't believe that everything I believe in, out there, is coming to an end!"

"We don't know."

"Maybe our children will burst out into the galaxy again. And find the worlds of the Inquestors. And heal the wounds, maybe." She smiled at him in the alien moonlight. There was a moment of fierce, burning pride. Then—

"Look!" she cried suddenly.

His eyes followed the curve of her arm, up into the blackness. A meteor flashed. Fireworks. The sand glittered silver for a moment. The hills glowed and faded. "It's the ship," he said. "It's the past, burning up as it hits the atmosphere. "

"Happy?"

"I suppose so…"

The moon hid in a cloud, and in the darkness the only light was the cold clingfire of her dress. *We'll have to make our own warmth.*

They pressed closer together. Ahead, the plain was full of. their unborn children, waiting to be created. They held each other close, not only for the warmth now. The first step into the future waited to be taken.

And then they took it.

The first step was a kiss, an embrace, an act of love.

Spectacle!

a modest introduction

by Darrell Schweitzer

I have before me my copy of the first edition of this book. It is autographed, with an inscription that reads:

> *To Darrell,*
> *With Spectacle*
> > *Ludic*
> *Bhakti*
> *Bap*
> *and CounTERculture*
> > *Somtow.*

That takes a certain amount of explanation, but it does remind me that I have admired Somtow Sucharitkul (or. S.P. Somtow as he became known to the literary world) for somewhat over forty years now, which means we are both now vigorous and energetic seniors, whereas in the old days we were somewhat less senior, and Somtow at least seemed to be frantically energetic and creative.

I also have a copy of his first story collection, *Fire from the Wine Dark Sea*, which was published by the Donning Company in 1983. I was published by the Donning Company in 1983 too, so in this sense we were colleagues, although I think Somtow was more of their A-list author. The editor of the line was convinced he was a genius, and time has done nothing to erase that judgment.

My copy of *Fire from the Wine Dark Sea* is inscribed to me in the High Script of the Inquest. I have no idea what it says now.   That may require a bit more explanation.

The Donning Company was something of a second-string outfit. It was impressive enough that I could get published by them (a story-cycle disguised as a novel and an actual novel), but they began with a short-story collection by Somtow because he was already a big name. He had won the John W. Campbell Award for best new writer. He already had two Hugo Award nominations.

So my primary publisher was his secondary publisher. His novels, starting with *Starship & Haiku* (1991), were published by Timescape, which, in those days Timescape was the flagship line for the science fiction field, the same imprint which brought Gene Wolfe's *The Book of the New Sun* out in mass-market paperback. It was the place to be noticed. David G.

Hartwell, who has responsible for discovering and nurturing a substantial amount of the top science fiction talent was the editor there.

I first came to know Somtow because I was working as an editorial assistant for George Scithers on *Isaac Asimov's Science Fiction Magazine* (a member of a team of several such, known collectively as "The Zoo"). By 1980 Somtow was a star contributor, one of the magazine's "big three," important new writers being heavily promoted by the magazine. (The other two were John M. Ford and Barry Longyear.) Somtow was always my favorite. I was amused and impressed by his "Mallworld" series, about a shopping mall in the outer solar system, where humans are overseen by the alien Selispridar, who have isolated the human race as unfit for galactic company, but have their own nasty foibles, such as that they eat millions of their own excess offspring like shrimp at a buffet as part of their normal life-cycle. *Mallworld* is full of great satire and humor, but also moments of pathos and real drama. It is not entirely silly. The silliness can ease you into much darker territory.

And now about "spectacle," "ludic," "bhakti," and "bap," which figure so prominently in that inscription cited above. These were some of the bywords of what can only be called Somtow Mania, a phenomenon quite evident in science fiction fan circles in the early 1980s. Think of the Beatles and the word "gear." Sort of like that. 1964 or 1965 was "a gear year." Remember that? You didn't necessarily know what it meant, but it got repeated. Somtow as a celebrity and personality was one of the most entertaining people in science fiction at the time, and what he said got repeated. A famous wit. He could draw a crowd at conventions simply of people who wanted to hear what he had to say or watch what he did, so they could tell a Somtow story later on. Harlan Ellison was like that too, although Harlan got into fights and controversies all the time. Somtow did not. Everybody liked Somtow. Back in the days when desktop computers were still a novelty and if someone brought one to a convention it would draw its own audience, Somtow proudly demonstrated how he'd induced a music program on an early MacIntosh to clash with itself until he made it fart. The climax of such hijinks came with the Sucharitkul in 1980 campaign, in which he mockingly pretended to run for the John W. Campbell Award (for best new writer) as if it were a political election. There were bid parties. There were children wandering the corridors of convention hotels wearing sandwich-board signs saying "VOTE SUCHARITKUL IN '80." I still have my campaign button. Even more clever and witty than that was the fact that he admitted in an interview I did with him at the time that the "inner insidiousness" of the whole thing was that he did not expect to win, but the "joke" would get him attention. Then, he did not intend to campaign in 1981, his last year of eligibility, and therefore might win on the "pity vote." What was supremely clever was that this actually worked.

So, while Somtow established himself as a celebrity in science fiction, this frivolous and tacky exterior only semi-concealed and actually drew your attention to his greater depths. Even as those Mallworld stories were more than just jokes, Somtow has always been more than a jester. For one thing, he continues to have a significant musical career, as a composer and conductor. He has written operas. (He also wrote, at George Scithers's behest, "The Isaac Asimov's Science Fiction Magazine March.") But if you look at the Inquestor series, starting with the book you hold in your hands right now, you find something that is romantic and beautiful and strange, what Brian Aldiss once called "wide-screen baroque" science fiction, an imaginary universe of considerable complexity. Here we see a lot of characteristic Somtow touches. The heightened, poetic language. Sensitive, but not sentimental depictions of children characters. The theme of *Light on the Sound* is a discontent with the status quo which moves on to rebellion. His characters do the archetypal things that science fiction characters do, particularly young ones. They set out to discover how the universe really works, rather than just believe what their parents or tradition have told them. (Think of Arthur C. Clarke's *Against the Fall of Night*.)

We meet three such characters from three very different societies, none of whom are satisfied with their lot. One has a dull existence providing food for people of the "Dark Country" that he is not sure even exists. Another is a young girl who finds herself the only sighted and hearing person in the country of the blind and deaf. Her people live out their lives in darkness and in silence, their task being to kill and harvest "delphinoids," sort of air-whales that live in a vast, dark chasm, and produce songs and light-poems of such ineffable beauty that anyone who perceives them cannot return to being mere humans afterwards. The brains of the delphinoids make interstellar travel possible, which is the basis of the vast empire known as the Dispersal of Man. Incidentally, dead people from the Dark Country are recycled to feed the delphinoids. Overseeing all this is the ancient and all-powerful ruling caste of the Inquest, which as its stated mission seeks out and destroys utopias, since the whole setup depends on suffering. The third main character is one of the Inquestors, who also has come to question the traditional order of things and, after having disposed of twelve previous utopias, now may have found one he urgently wishes to preserve.

This is a more bizarre system than that of Frank Herbert's *Dune*. Imagine if David Lynch had filmed this instead.

Inevitably, probably because the ruling elite is called the Inquest, readers equate Somtow's universe with that of the SF master Cordwainer Smith, who wrote of the Instrumentality of Man and its Lords. In that same interview I did with him, Somtow expressed great admiration for Smith's work, but commented that his own universe is "less Oriental" than Smith's. Maybe so. Smith (real name Paul Linebarger) was a noted Asia scholar, a close confidant of Chiang Kai-shek, and the godson of Sun Yat-sen.

Somtow's universe is probably far more operatic than Smith's. I will let someone more musically literate than myself explore that. What his work has shown from the outset has been a genuinely different cultural perspective from that of most American science fiction writers. He was born in Bangkok, raised in several countries, educated in England (he went to Eton), and went back to Thailand early in his adulthood to learn the language and immerse himself in the culture. Thus he is able to write quite differently from someone who spent their whole life in a New Jersey suburb. His voice is distinctive. His imagination and talent are huge. His work is a genuine fusion of Asian and Western ideas.

It's great to see the Inquestor series re-issued, and to see Somtow writing more of these books.

You're going to like this series.

■ Darrell Schweitzer, April 30, 2020

The Good, the Bad, and the Ugnaught

Thoughts While Binge-Watching "The Mandalorian"

I was finally able to watch *The Mandalorian* recently in between moments of incredible personal and professional stress. And one of the best things about it, ironically, is that it doesn't contain a single original idea. I'm not praising with faint damns here — far from it — I am trying to explain why this series is so appealing, absorbing, and generally bingeworthy.

Alexander Pope said of great poetry that is "what oft was said, yet ne'er so well express'd." *The Mandalorian* is great because it uses tropes that we know and love, and serves them up in ways that are fresh and surprising enough to please the palate and push our emotional buttons. Everyone knows apples and walnuts — yet a Waldorf salad is an exquisite masterpiece of recombinant DNA.

And when you start disassembling the tropes, you also see a whole history of science fiction and adventure stories — a long line stretching all the way back to Gilgamesh, but this is just a short review so I'll mostly stick with the last hundred years.

First, it's the music the telegraphs the milieu. Gone are the lush late-romantic soundscapes of "big epic".   Odd, ethnic sounding wind instruments, rattling percussion immediately bring a particular shade of Ennio Morricone to mind, so before we even see much, we know we're in a sort of spaghetti western.   The lone hero travelling through a desert with a mute child is also inhabiting the world of Jodorowsky's *El Topo* ... and then there's the veneer of orientalism — the ronin-like guild, "the way" (and what is the way but *bushido?).* We are in a very real sense back in the 1970s, the "birth time" of *Star Wars* — but we have moved in the direction of David Carradine in *Kung Fu* — a TV series so influential to the culture and to

what came after that we take all its radical influences for granted and have forgotten the show itself.

All of this puts us in the same universe as *Star Wars* but in a wholly "new" kind of "old" story — the picaresque tale of a knight errant on a solitary quest accompanied by a mysterious fifty-year-old Child.

Calling the companion simply "The Child" and mentioning its age reminds us also The Child, one of the main Jungian archetypes, isn't just some undeveloped person but in mythological terms is someone infinitely old and wise who *appears* as a Child.

So, apart from a few red herrings in the middle, this is a pretty clean clear-cut arc of a story and I am not surprised that it's getting more positive attention than the more ambiguous and perhaps "kit-bashed" films of the final trilogy. The Mandalorian with his thinly disguised *bushido* code, the miniature Yoda-like alien, the much subtler *fansaabisu* which reference more obscure minutiae of the canon (and occasionally even things rejected from canon) ... all these things keep hitting the right buttons and it's particularly delicious that this iteration of the "hero with a thousand faces" has no face.

Indeed, how any acting manages to occur at all is a triumph with all that armor. I am assuming its mostly ADR work, meaning that scenes of interactions with others must be particularly hard on the other actors. And yet it kind of works. Perhaps a "Lone Hero" by nature *has* to act like a block of wood — *pace* David Carradine. The inevitable last minute face revelation, mandated by the structure of such shows, was almost unnecessary, though it was useful to see that the hero was not some scarred monster — or some surprise celebrity — as men in iron masks are wont to be

Although it's clear that "Baby Yoda" has injected an almost unbearable level of cuteness into the show, this little guy's no Ewok. The Ewoks were somewhat nauseating in their cuteness whereas B.Y. is genuinely adorable. The Ewoks were very obviously toys, as well, and served no actual plot-based purpose, whereas the existence of the B.Y. opens all sorts of doors and asks interesting questions. And puppetry, or whatever this is, seems to have improved a lot since the Ewoks — whose toy-ness one could never actually forget. B.Y. was pretty convincing — this was no muppet.

The best thing about this new series is the very human scale in which it's set. There aren't any space battles with thousands of battleships, and there isn't a super-weapon that annihilates an entire planet, let alone an entire fleet of such weapons. There's no one who wants to rule the entire universe — just a planet or two is fine. As befits climbing down from the movie screen to the home screen, the operatic bombast is greatly reduced.

When an actor plays one of those rugged, implacable types, we often say that his face is masklike. In *The Mandalorian,* the face and the mask are one, so acting ability is basically moot. Sexual charisma is moot. Rippling muscles are moot. Hell, it's *all* moot. The ability to play a convincing protagonist while completely encased in Beskar is probably quite rare, though we don't have many antecedents to compare our favorite bounty hunter with. Dav:d Carradine probably worked pretty hard to impersonate a block of wood; portraying a hunk of metal comes easy to Pedro Pascal, thanks to the fact that he *is* his costume.

And yet we're all in love with him.

It doesn't hurt that we were in love with Boba Fett when ˙1e was no more than an action figure. It doesn't hurt that Baby Yoda presumably sees his saintly nature beneath his rough-hewn exterior — presumably being a Force user lets you see the man beneath the metal.

So — it's the adventures of a tin man and a cute puppet, zooming through the galaxy, busting balls. one step ahead of the law, bargaining with jawas, getting chased through sewers, with a healthy dose of scum and villainy — how could one not enjoy it, guilty pleasure though it might be? And when the wicked Moff pulls out a — gasp — *darksaber* — while our hero fir.ally achieves flight — well, a lot of buttons are being pushed.

It's not *deep,* as such, but there's enough quasi-Eastern philosophy woven into it to create a credible aura of depth. And it asks many questions that Warsies have always wanted answers to. Next season, presumably, there will be answers.

The Inquestor Series

The Novels

Light on the Sound (1982)
The Throne of Madness (1983)
Utopia Hunters (1984)
The Darkling Wind   (1985)
Homeworld of the Heart (2020)

Inquestor Tales (in process)
   Part One: *The Singing Moons* (2018)
   Part Two: *A Woman Cloaked in Shadow (2018)*
   Part Three: *The Child Collector (2019)*
   Part Four: *The Space Between Spaces (2020)*
   Part Five: *Goddess in the Ruins (2020)*

in process
Vara's World
Stillness in Starlight

The Short Stories

The Thirteenth Utopia (Analog, 1979)
The Web Dancer (IASFM, 1979)
Darktouch (IASFM, 1980) (non-canonical)
Light on the Sound (IASFM, 1980)
The Rainbow King (IASFM, 1981)
The Dust (IASFM, 1981)
Remembrances (IASFM, 1982)
Scarlet Snow (IASFM, 1982)
The Comet that Cried for its Mother (Amazing, 1984)